BETWEEN *Us*

the SEX ON THE BEACH series

BETWEEN *Us*

the SEX ON THE BEACH series

Jen McLaughlin

Manufactured in the United States of America
ISBN: 978-0-9896684-3-9

The author acknowledges the copyrighted or trademarked status and trademark owners of the following wordmarks mentioned in this work of fiction: Pretty Woman, Maker's Mark, Hinder, Google, iPhone, Redskins, TMZ, Volkswagen, Margaritaville, Mac Air, ET, E! News, E!, Smarty Jones, FaceTime, and Nicholas Sparks.

Photo by: Pamela Mullins
Edited by: Kristin at Coat of Polish Edits
Copy edited by: Hollie Westring
Cover Designed by: Sarah Hansen at © OkayCreations.net
Interior Design and Formatting by: E.M. Tippetts Book Designs

Dear Reader,

Prepare yourself for Sex on the Beach, a trilogy featuring BETWEEN US (Jen McLaughlin), BEYOND ME (Jennifer Probst), and BEFORE YOU (Jenna Bennett). Three separate novellas. Three different authors. One literary world. Read them all, or just read one. It's up to you! No matter which route you choose, these standalone novellas are sure to satisfy your need for sizzling romance and an emotion packed story.

Happy Reading!
Jen, Jenna, and Jennifer

Praise for BETWEEN US:

"The sweet good-girl looking to be a bit naughty and the sexy bad-boy looking to be thought of as good…Jen gives us another winning story with BETWEEN US. Drool worthy and devourable with plenty of emotion, I adored this book from start to finish! A must read!" *–Jillian, from Read, Love, Blog*

"Anything that Jen McLaughlin writes is gold, in my book. BETWEEN US is no different. Set in the sweltering heat of Key West, it has all the passion, friendship and drama that made it impossible to put down. Go read this book. You won't be disappointed!" *–Casey, Literary Escapism*

Praise for BEYOND ME:

"I loved this book, I very much enjoyed getting to know James and Quinn, and I wanted to step into their world of sun and water and love. This book made spring break even more fun, even with the intense feelings, I want to head to Florida now! I give this book 5 huge sunny and sandy stars!" *–Sizzling Book Blog*

"Jennifer Probst does it again in Beyond Me with another amazing hit. From the first chapter I was captivated immediately and couldn't put it down. The chemistry between James and Quinn had my heart racing, soaring, and dropping on more than one occasion. I found myself lost in their story, not wanting it to end." *–NYT & USA Today Bestselling Author Kelly Elliott*

Praise for BEFORE YOU:

"The story felt fun, as Cassie enjoys the sunshine, and things develop and start to sizzle when she meets Ty. It kept me on the edge of my seat...and I was curling my toes at the romance." *–Bella, from A Prairie Girl Reads*

"A thrilling mystery mixed with romance and some much needed humor and wittiness, Before You is an enjoyable and gripping story." *–Stella, Ex Libris*

I'm just a girl...

I'm a famous country star who's spent her life cultivating a good girl persona to avoid bad press, but I've reached my limit. I'm going away for spring break with my two best friends from college, and we've vowed to spend the vacation seeking out fun in the sun—along with some hot, no-strings-attached sex. The only thing I needed was the perfect guy, and then I met Austin Murphy. He might be totally wrong for me, but the tattooed bad boy is hard to resist. When I'm in his arms, everything just feels *right*.

And I'm just a guy...

I'm just a bartender who lives in Key West, stuck in an endless cycle of boredom. But then Mackenzie Forbes, America's Sweetheart herself, comes up to me and looks at me with those bright green eyes...and everything changes. She acts like she's just a normal girl and I'm just a normal guy, but that couldn't be further from the truth. My past isn't pretty, you know. I did what I had to do to survive, and she'd run if she learned the truth about my darkness. But with her, I'm finally realizing what it's like to be *alive*. To laugh, live, and be happy.

All good things must come to an end..

To Jenna and Jennifer—It's been such a pleasure working with both of you! Thank you for being so amazing, and so much fun to work with!

CHAPTER

Mackenzie

The salsa music blaring in the background almost made up for the fact that it was over ninety degrees outside and I was melting, but the Sex on the Beach in my hand? Well, that totally made up for any residual heat that was frizzing my curly hair, Chia Pet style, and the fine sheen of sweat covering my body.

Now, I needed to work up a sweat in a different way.

This was what I'd wanted when I dragged my best friends, Quinn and Cassie, down here for an impromptu spring break in Key West. We'd debated going somewhere else for more privacy, or maybe renting a private home or something, but Key West was the ultimate spring break spot, and with the hordes of bodies shoved into any one building, the chances of me being recognized down here were slim to none.

With any luck, I'd blend right in. I'd even dyed my hair and refused to allow any security to come along. We wanted the ultimate spring break experience—and this was the best way to get it. By me trying to be normal for once.

For this one short, glorious week, I was a normal girl. For the next few days, I'd have my besties at my side, the sun over our heads, the warm sand between our toes, the fruity booze on our tongues, and the warm water beckoning for us to come in. The only thing missing was my spring fling, but I hadn't found a guy who fit my requirements. I'd been looking since we arrived yesterday afternoon, but no luck so far. I was a little bit picky when it came to men…

Okay, a *lot* picky. So sue me.

When you're a famous country star—the same one who'd been dubbed "America's Sweetheart" the moment you first appeared on stage—you had a certain criteria for men. And one of the most important ones that was non-negotiable?

Absolutely, positively *no* talking to paparazzi afterward.

It was a heck of a lot harder than you'd think to find a man who wouldn't sell you out after making you scream his name. Trust me. I've *tried* to find one, and failed. It's why I was still a virgin. But after this trip, I wouldn't be. I was going to find the right guy. Someone who wouldn't know who I was, so there would be no messy complications afterward.

And I had my eyes on him *now*.

Cassie nudged me in the ribs. "Are you sleeping under that huge hat or what?"

"Of course not." I tugged my sun hat lower, peeking over my shoulder as I did so. "I'm just man-hunting is all. You should be, too. We agreed we'd all get laid this weekend."

"I'm looking." Cassie took a sip of her drink, her blonde hair sparkling under the twinkling lights overhead. "Kinda."

"Are we still splitting up as much as possible?" Quinn asked.

"Yeah, we have to. It's why we have separate rooms. We won't get laid if we're two to a bed." I looked at the guy at the bar again. I needed an excuse to get up there. "Are you girls ready for a refill yet?"

They'd decorated the outside bar with white lights all over, and tiny little lanterns hung from the wood ceiling beams overhead. "I can't down them like there's no tomorrow. Something tells me a hospital visit is *not* on your spring break agenda," Cassie said.

I pointed at her with my drink, concern for their safety taking over. Maybe we shouldn't split up. What if something happened to one of them? I'd die. "Absolutely not. Watch how much you drink. Balance it out with water at all times, never accept a drink from a stranger, and we have to make sure to keep in contact via text at least a few times a day, so we know we're all okay."

"We already knew that," Quinn said, her soft voice crystal clear. Her long, dark hair was flawless, as usual, and her dark eyes narrowed on me. "We got the usual Mackenzie speech the whole way down."

"I don't give speeches…okay, never mind. I totally do."

Cassie rolled her eyes and Quinn snorted. I fought the urge to hug them tight, but that was nothing new. I always felt that way around them. Grateful they accepted me as I was. Happy we'd met. You know, all those mushy-gushy feelings that I threw into my music but never really voiced out loud.

They were the only ones who didn't treat me like I was different because I was famous. It had been a refreshing change of pace, to say the least. We'd bonded two years ago in English 101 when I'd asked Cassie what a dangling participle was, and Quinn had answered from Cassie's other side. We'd been inseparable ever since. I still didn't know what a dangling participle was, but that was okay.

I had them. And soon I'd have *him*.

I pulled my sun hat lower and continued to scope out the guy at the bar. He wasn't looking this way, so I feasted my eyes on his utter hotness. He had dark brown hair, and I was pretty sure I spotted a chin dimple from over here. His arms were inked up, and he oozed sexual confidence without even trying.

He was probably about six-foot-one, and he had the kind of muscles that showed he worked out, but he didn't look overly big like those wrestlers or bodybuilders. He was perfection. Something about the way he held himself and the way he carried on a conversation spoke of a confidence a girl like me could appreciate. He looked like he knew what to do inside the bedroom *and* out of it, and that's what I needed tonight.

"Girls?" I leaned in closer, and they did, too. "I think I found my guy. Ten o'clock. Black shirt and brown hair."

Quinn peeked while taking a casual sip of her drink. "Hmm. He's promising. But he kind of looks…dangerous."

He did, and I liked that about him. It was the right style of dangerous he oozed—not the "tie me up in a basement and kill me" type.

"Yeah, I don't know about him, Mac." Cassie's brow furrowed. "He's tapping his foot to the music way too perfectly. He's got to be a musician. And all that ink? He's hardly your type."

Oh, he's totally my type. I watched his foot move. Seeing him in perfect rhythm with the music was a huge turn-on for me. As a musician, I couldn't help but be attracted to men who could carry a tune or a beat.

And this dude? Yeah, he had it.

"Hm. Maybe he's a little dangerous, but I like that about him." I took a deeper drink, needing the coolness to cool off my overheated cheeks. "And why is him being a musician such a bad thing?"

"Because he might recognize you and sell out for a quick buck," Cassie said, her gray eyes twinkling. She looked halfway to toasted already, and we were only on our first Sex on the Beach. "It wouldn't be the first time. Need I remind you of what happened when you almost slept with that guy from the club back in Chicago? You didn't even seal the deal, so to speak, and the press ate you alive. Do you want to be role model turned Slutty McSluttergans all over again?"

I flinched. "It's not fair. I'm a virgin, but the one time I appear in the tabloids, I'm a huge whore?" I took a deep sip, my eyes still on the guy at the bar. "Well, screw them. Besides, I dyed my hair and I'm wearing this big hat. No one will know it's me."

Cassie blinked at me, looking way too worried for someone who was supposed to be having fun. "Your brown hair isn't all that different from your blonde, Mac."

"It's the best I could do." I'd considered multiple wigs and big glasses, but that would look weird. And it kind of felt too *Pretty Woman* to me. "I'm going in."

Cassie looked at him again. "But are you sure he's the right guy to do it?"

"Yep." I finished off my drink and stood, the empty glass in my hand. "Wish me luck."

"Good luck," Quinn called.

Cassie smiled. "You don't need it. Just be careful. And thank you again for bringing us here."

"It's nothing," I said. "See ya soon."

An all-expenses paid vacation was the least I could do for them, when they'd done so much for me. It's not as if I couldn't afford it or anything. They weren't as blessed as me financially, so I paid for them to come with me. That's all there was to it.

I don't think they really understood how much it meant to me to have two best friends I could count on for anything. They wouldn't steal from me or betray me like my mom had. I flinched at the thought. I tried not to think about her.

It had taken five months for my father to realize there was missing money in my bank account. It had taken less than twenty-four hours to figure out why. It had gone into my mother's pockets—and up her nose—while we'd been away from home. After we figured out she was a junkie, there had been a big, sloppy, public divorce, and everyone had felt sorry for me.

I'd been seventeen and stuck between two warring parents. We'd managed to hide the drug aspect of the story from the tabloids during the court proceedings, but God only knows how. I didn't speak to her anymore—she hadn't even come to Dad's funeral. As far as I knew, she was still a junkie and always would be. Money had corrupted her soul. I would never let it do the same to mine.

I'd been extremely careful to keep my image squeaky clean ever since. My father had been adamant I had to make sure I did no wrong in the eyes of the media. That way if the truth ever came out about Mom, I'd still be the good one in their eyes. Never step out of line. Never get caught doing something bad. And never misbehave in public.

He'd died in a car crash two years ago, but I still lived by those rules of his.

I didn't know any other way.

As I made my way over to the guy at the bar, making sure to swing my hips *just so* to attract his attention, I lowered my head. I might be a virgin, but I'd won *Who Sings It Best* at fifteen, and I'd been starring in music videos since I was sixteen. And what was in music videos? Sex, sex, and more sex. It might not be actual sex, but it was all about the approach and the hotness factor. And I had that down pat, so I could totally fake the rest. It was all in the confidence.

Even if the confidence was fake.

His gaze skimmed over me the closer I got. He adjusted his position on the barstool so he was turned slightly toward me. I knew this guy at the bar was the type of guy to fit into my strict plans. I could feel it in my bones, the same feeling I got when I played the right chord or heard a song that I had to sing.

It just fit.

"This seat taken?" I asked, my country drawl a little bit more obvious with a drink or two already in me.

He gestured at it with his left hand. "Please. Sit."

I scooted up onto the stool, stealing a quick peek at him from under my hat as I did so. I eyed his ink, making out a few foreign words in bright colors, and some black swirls inked around the words. Flames too.

Hot. Really hot.

"Thank you," I said, motioning toward the bartender. He came over and smiled at me. "I'll have another Sex on the Beach, and I'd like two more for the table over there." I pointed at my girls, waving at them to show that I knew them. They waved back, then whispered to each other. I turned back to my guy. "And another of whatever he's having."

He cocked a brown brow. "Do you always order for other people?"

"Sometimes." I lifted my head slightly, still not making full eye contact thanks to my wide-brimmed hat. "I'm a girl who knows what she wants and goes after it. Is that going to be a problem?"

He laughed lightly, the sound musical. Oh, the girls had been right. I bet this guy could sing the dress off an angel. "No, that won't be a problem. I'll have two fingers of Maker's Mark, please."

I handed my card to the bartender. "Ah, so you're a whiskey guy? Before he died, my daddy always used to tell me to find a man who could appreciate the finer things in life." I deepened my voice. "'Find a man who can sit back and enjoy the sunset and the way the waves roll over the beach on a stormy day. And he should also appreciate things like whiskey and Cuban cigars.'"

"They're illegal," the man on the barstool said, leaning closer. "But I do enjoy a good Cuban. Sunsets and the ocean, too."

I flushed, my stomach tightening at the way he'd dropped his voice. This guy was affecting me in ways I'd never felt before. "Good to know you like breaking the rules every once in a while."

He laughed again, his fingers clutching his glass. All I could see of him, due to my hat, was his hand and his legs, which were encased in torn blue jeans. Because of this, I could just barely make out the dark hair on his thigh. "You have *no* idea."

"Oh, I bet I do."

He tapped the side of his glass with his finger. "Pardon me for being rude, but can you lose the hat?" He reached out and tugged on it gently, trying to remove it but not being forceful. "I can't even see your face."

I held onto the brim of the hat, keeping it in place. "Maybe that's the point."

"The hat goes or I go." He rested a hand on my thigh. My dress stopped right at the knee, so he wasn't touching bare skin, but he might as well have been for the impact it had on me. I quivered. Yes, *quivered*. "I don't play games. You're either in or you're out in my world. Is that going to be a problem?"

I waited too long to answer. He sighed and started to remove his hand from my leg, intending to leave. I panicked, knowing nothing except that I couldn't let this guy walk away from me. Not yet. So I covered his hand with mine, holding it firmly in place. "Fine, but first tell me what you sing."

"What? How did you...?" He tensed. "Have we met before?"

I shook my head. "No, I just have a feeling you're a singer."

"Well, you're right." He hesitated. "I mostly sing rock. My style is similar to Hinder, I guess. Hell, I even share a first name with the former lead singer." He tugged on the hat again. "Now lose the hat, sweetheart."

I took a deep breath, said a quick prayer he wouldn't know who I was—or that if he did, he wouldn't sell me out—and then pulled off the hat. The second I looked up at him, I made eye contact, dying to know what color eyes he had. Turned out, he had the brightest blue eyes fringed with the darkest lashes I'd ever seen.

He stared back at me, making my breath hitch in my throat. And I'd been right. He had a dimple in his chin that begged for me to touch it. The dimple gave him a boyish charm, which contrasted with the sharp cheekbones that made him look hardened. He had a scar on his cheekbone, and his nose looked as if it had been broken once or twice, and he was simply…devastatingly *hot*. That was the best way to describe him.

And beyond that? He called to my very soul.

I almost laughed at the sappy thought. I mean, sure, I sang about love and heartbreak all the time. But the truth was, I could count on one hand how many actual boyfriends I'd had. And most of them were in grade school when I'd been flat-chested and buck-toothed.

I might sing about love and romance and finding the one, but I wouldn't know what love was if it hit me square in the face. Heck, I wasn't even sure if I really believed in love at all. But this guy? This one dude?

He made me want to believe.

CHAPTER

Austin

oly shit. I couldn't believe my luck. I couldn't believe that I had none other than Mackenzie Forbes, America's *fucking* Sweetheart, flirting with me as if she was just a normal girl and I was a normal guy. Well, the second part was true. I was a normal guy, but she was most definitely not a normal girl.

She'd dyed her hair brown. It was usually a bright and sunny blonde. Was that part of her disguise, in addition to the hat she had been wearing? It had worked for a while. I'd had no idea who she was until she looked up at me. But if she knew who she was talking to, she wouldn't be here right now.

If she knew who I was, what I'd done, and where I'd been, she wouldn't be batting those famous green eyes at me, looking as if she wanted nothing more outta the world than me. Seriously, I was almost as far from her type as you could possibly get. Actually, one could easily say that my whole life had been filled with almosts…

I *almost* graduated high school, but then ran away. I *almost* killed my father when he beat my younger sister instead of me. Oh, and I *almost* went to jail for *almost* killing said father. And to top it off? I *almost* got a recording deal, but I lost it when I *almost* went to jail for *almost* killing my father.

Yeah. Like I said. Lots of almosts.

I'd been sitting here, wishing I could catch a fucking break for once in my life, and then *bam*. Mackenzie Forbes lands in my lap. Back in California, I used to take pictures of celebrities. The whole thing had felt dirty and soul-suckingly horrible, but it had paid the bills while I'd tried to get my career in music up and running. It had been years since I sold a picture to the media.

And yet, all it would take was a couple pictures of her, and a tabloid willing to pay for them, and I'd be able to buy groceries for a month. Hell, if I could get some pictures or a video of her in a compromising position or two, I could probably afford a decent place to live.

I couldn't *not* take advantage of that…could I?

But then again, I'd quit taking pictures of celebrities for a reason. I didn't like the way it made me feel afterward—all sleazy and gross. I didn't want to be that guy anymore, damn it. But the money…

I forced a lighthearted smile, trying to act normal. I didn't want to spook her before I decided what to do with her. I had a feeling a girl like her strived for anonymity in things like this, and who was I not to give it to her? I tried to remember everything I knew about her. She'd been on one of those talent shows, I think. Sang her way to the winning position and had been at the top of the charts ever since.

And now she was here with me. Imagine that. I forced a smile. "That's much better. You've got a pretty face, sweetheart."

Wait, should I not call her that? Would it make her think I knew who she was? I mean, I did know, but I didn't want her to know I knew.

She nibbled on her lower lip, her cheeks flushed. "You think?"

"Oh, yeah." I smiled and picked up my drink, trying to be casual and laid back, when inside I was strung tighter than a live wire. "I've seen a lot of pretty faces in my life, but you might be the winner."

Just like you won that singing competition on TV.

She relaxed slightly. She seemed to think I didn't recognize her. Was she really that gullible? It almost made me want to throw my arm over her shoulders and protect her from the big bad world. Protect her from assholes like me. That was irony at its finest, right there.

"Thank you." She picked up her drink and took a sip, her pink lips closing around the straw perfectly. "Your face is pretty spectacular, too. Just for the record."

I chuckled at the casual compliment. "Thanks."

We fell silent, each watching the other. I couldn't figure out what she wanted from me. Out of all the people in this bar…why me? My phone buzzed and I pulled it out, quickly scanning the text. After I finished, I flipped my phone over so she couldn't see the screen, and took another sip. My old junker of a phone looked ridiculous next to her shiny iPhone.

Kinda like how *we* must look right now.

"So, what brings a girl like you to Key West?" I asked.

"Spring break." She tipped her head toward the table where her friends had been sitting. "I'm here with my friends, just chilling. We go to the University of Chicago. Decided some warmth would be nice."

Did she actually go to college? If so, what a waste of time. She'd probably already made millions singing. Why bother paying for an education after all that? She already had a lucrative career. And how did that work, exactly? Didn't she need security with her at all times? Hell, maybe they were here right now.

I had so many fucking questions, and I couldn't ask a single one. "Well, you came to the right place. It's always hot here."

"I know, and I *love* it." Her gaze dipped low, running over my tats on my arms. I knew she was probably drooling over them. Good girls like her loved getting close to a bad boy with ink like me. It probably made them feel as if they'd walked on the dark side and survived, or some shit like that. For the most part, I didn't mind playing that role for a little bit of fun. "Do you live down here?"

I tapped my fingers on my knee absentmindedly. "I do."

"Have you always lived here?"

I tossed back the rest of my drink and let out a soft chuckle. "Nope."

"Where are you from?"

She motioned the bartender over and pointed at my drink, smiling at the man and pulling out a twenty. I stiffened. I didn't need her to buy all my fucking drinks. I could take care of my own responsibilities and myself. I'd been doing it since I was seventeen.

It might not have always come easy, but I made ends meet.

"Around." I reached out, slid her money back in front of her, and threw down my own. "And I've got this round."

She blinked at me. "I can pay for your drink. I want to."

"I've got it," I repeated, catching her gaze. "I'm good."

She stared at me, as if no one had ever told her no before. Hell, no one probably had. If I recalled correctly, she was an only child and her parents were out of the picture. One might have been dead…that father she'd mentioned earlier, more than likely.

Her parents had gotten a divorce, and there had been a big custody battle over her when she was a kid. Didn't sound like a very charmed life, but it was a fucking fairytale compared to mine.

Barry brought me another drink, along with another for her, and I nodded at him. He gave me a long look, took my twenty, and walked away. I knew he wanted to know what the hell I was doing with such a fresh-faced girl like Mackenzie

Forbes, but I didn't have an answer for that yet. "How long are you staying here in Key West?"

She swallowed the last of her drink and started the next. The girl was obviously looking to get plastered and get laid. I had a feeling that's where I came in. But I didn't screw drunk girls. It felt like taking advantage to me, no matter how willing they were before the drinks.

"I'll be here through Saturday." She turned to me, her knees brushing my thigh. The simple touch burned through my jeans, as if she was stroking me instead of touching me innocently. Fuck me, this girl was good. "Want to keep me company?"

I cleared my throat and took a long drink. She didn't mess around. "Aren't I doing that right now?" I vaguely remembered some rumors about her being caught with a drummer inside a club in Chicago, but I couldn't remember the details. I'd have to Google it later. "Keeping you company?"

"I'm going to be one hundred percent forthright right now." She met my eyes, her fingers drifting over my tats lightly. It did weird things to my body—her touch on my skin. "I'm looking for some harmless, no-strings-attached fun tonight. What do you think about that?"

I laughed uneasily and shifted my weight on the stool. My cock thickened at her words and her touch, but I ignored the urge to take her up on her offer. The girl was plastered, plain and simple. No matter how tempted I was, it wouldn't be happening tonight. "Out of curiosity, how many of those fruity drinks have you had?"

"It's called Sex on the Beach," she said, dipping her voice low and biting down on her lower lip in a mockery of innocence. This girl might play sweet and innocent in the public eye, but she was too good to be *that* innocent. "I figured it was only right, since that's exactly what I wanted out of tonight. Sex." She paused, then added, "Maybe on the beach." As if it needed clarification? "So...you in or not?"

She was a smart girl, turning my own words back around

on me like that. "You didn't answer my question," I said, sliding her drink out of reach. "How many drinks?"

Across the bar, I saw one of her friends chatting with some guy I vaguely recognized. He watched me closely, as if he knew I didn't belong with a girl like Mackenzie. He was right, of course. But he didn't know me, so I shot him a narrow-eyed look that told him to mind his own fucking business. He didn't look away immediately.

Was he Mackenzie's security guard or something?

"Um, two, I think?" she said, pulling my attention back to where it belonged. Then she shrugged. "But I wanted you before I started drinking."

"Look…I'm not sure—"

"Oh. Okay." She stood up unsteadily, her cheeks bright red, but she stared me down, as if she refused to acknowledge the hurt pride my rejection caused her. "Thanks for letting me down nicely. I'll just, uh…" She lifted a hand, then let it fall to her side. "Yeah. I'll just go find someone else to hit on and leave you alone."

The hell she would. That wasn't happening. I stood up and offered her my hand. "I'm in. Let's go."

"N-Now?" she squeaked, looking at her full drink with a touch of desperation. She cleared her throat and gave me a seductive smile. It looked as fake as half the tits in this room. "I mean, uh, great. Your place or mine?"

No way in hell she was going to my place. "We'll go back to your room," I said, grabbing my phone and then her hand. "Where are you staying?"

She grinned. "At the Cove Suites."

Of course she was. It was the fanciest joint around, complete with penthouse suites. It was only a three-minute walk from here, more or less. "I see."

She picked up her hat and waved at her friend. The little blonde grinned and gave two thumbs up. Mackenzie set her hat back down on her head and linked her hand with mine. I could feel the dude I thought I recognized watching me, but I ignored him. He had to be her private security or something. Well, if so, he could fucking relax. She would be going to bed alone tonight. That's not to say she would be doing the same thing tomorrow. Tomorrow was a whole other ballgame.

Hell, if she wanted to have some fun, no-strings-attached sex…

I was her guy. It's the only kind of sex I let myself have for numerous reasons. But if it happened, she would be sober for it. End of story. I led her toward the hotel, my hand gripping hers tightly. "What's your name, anyway? You never told me."

"I'm…" She hesitated, as if she wasn't sure whether to lie to me, and then she seemed to decide. "I'm Mackenzie. You?"

So, she gave me half the truth. She just left off the last name.

"Austin. Austin Murphy."

She nodded. "I like that name."

"Thanks." It was the only thing my father ever gave me that I'd kept. Well, that and the scar on my cheekbone I'd gotten when he'd hit me with a broken beer bottle. I couldn't get rid of that either. "What's your major?"

I asked more as conversation filler than anything, but part of me was genuinely curious. Why in the world would a woman with the money and talent she had choose to go to college, of all places? She didn't need an education. Not with the voice she had.

"Psychology."

I cocked a brow. "Why?"

"Why not?" She laughed. "I like the human mind. It works in weird ways no one can quite understand. I thought it might help me get closer to understanding, though. It fascinates me."

I nodded. That made sense. It would probably help with writing emotional songs, if she wrote her own music. "I get that."

"Are you a student?"

I snorted. "Nope."

"Oh. How old are you?"

"I'm twenty-four. You?"

She paused. "Twenty-one."

Yeah, I knew that. But I couldn't admit it, could I? It didn't feel right, not letting her know I knew who she was. Maybe I'd tell her. Come clean and let her do what she wanted with that. Then again, maybe not. "Cool."

"So what was your major?"

I hadn't *had* a major. I'd been too busy chasing a dream to think about getting an education, and now it was too late for me. I fought hard to keep food on the table and a roof over my head, and on top of that, I had responsibilities and duties.

But I didn't want to admit that to her. Didn't want to tell her I barely had enough freedom to grab a fucking drink after work, let alone the luxury of a fancy education.

"I didn't go to college." I shrugged. "It's not my scene. I'm a bartender at the bar you were at. I finished my shift before you came, then I sang a few songs for an extra couple of bucks. That's what I do."

"Oh." She blinked at me. "But with your voice, I bet you could do so much more."

"You've never even heard me sing."

She stared straight ahead, her cheeks turning red. "Doesn't matter. I can tell."

"Well, I don't do anything besides bartend and sing for fun." I grinned at her, even though I didn't feel like smiling. The woman was hitting on all my weaknesses and failures without even blinking an eye. "I keep myself busy between the two. It's good enough for me."

She shook her head, obviously not able to understand. "I bet you could hit it big if you tried. Have you ever thought about it?"

It kind of freaked me out that she kept going on and on about my potential. Sure, once upon a time, I'd agreed with her. I'd thought I could be more than that guy with the abusive father who'd ruined him. Then life had gotten in the way, and I'd stopped trying to change myself. I'd always been, and always would be, just me.

And I was okay with that now. She might not understand, but it was true. I didn't want fame and fortune. "I'm fine like I am. I'm a bartender, and I'm cool with that. I sing for fun, and I'm cool with that. Will that be a problem for you?"

Ha. She wasn't the only one who could turn a person's words around on them.

She blinked at me. "No, but—"

I stopped walking and swung her into the alley right next to her hotel. I pressed her up against the concrete wall, trapping her in with my body. Before we set foot inside that hotel, we needed to get a few things straight.

She took a deep breath, all shaky, and tilted her head back so she could look up at me. "A-Austin?"

I pressed against her, showing her how badly I wanted her. I lowered my head and stopped when my lips were barely touching her ear. "This isn't about saving me from myself, or even about changing my life. It's about you and me having some fun, remember?"

She nodded frantically, her nails digging into my shoulders. "Y-Yes. I remember."

"Good." I nibbled on the side of her neck, just hard enough to sting. "Now here's how it's going to be. If you still want me tomorrow, I'll make you come so many times you'll never be able to look at a bed…or a beach, if that's what you want, without thinking about me. But not till tomorrow."

"But—" she said, but cut off when I rocked my hips into hers, lifting her leg slightly so I fit easily against her in all the right places. She whimpered and leaned her head against the wall, her eyes closing. "O…kay. But why tomorrow?"

"I want to be sure you want this." I flicked my tongue over her racing pulse. "And if you do, you'll have me. I'll be yours for the day, and then you can walk away with a clear conscience. Don't worry, I won't try to stop you. It will be pure, simple, scorching hot *sex.* Just you and me, any way you want me. Got it?"

She swallowed hard and gave a small nod. "Of course."

I nipped at her earlobe. "Good. Now what floor are you on?"

"The top one," she breathed.

I pushed off the wall, heading toward the elevator. Of course she'd be on the top floor. Only the penthouse for Mackenzie *fucking* Forbes. At some point, I'd come to a decision about what to do with her. I wouldn't be taking her picture, and I wouldn't be selling her out.

I'd be fucking her, plain and simple.

She swiped her card in the elevator lock, which allowed her access to the penthouse floor, and then we rode the elevator in silence, with her stealing quick glances at me every once in a while. I tried not to fidget. I'd hated small spaces ever since my father started locking me in dark closets when I was bad.

I was bad a lot, so you'd think I'd be immune to the fear by now, but that wasn't the case. I hated them, and I wanted out of the elevator. As I stood there, letting her look her fill, I stared right back at her. It couldn't be any clearer that I wasn't like *her* at all.

The elevator doors finally opened and we stepped out together. She smiled at me, and headed for the room to the left. I stopped her in front of it, my hand lightly gripping her elbow. She looked at me in surprise, her mouth a little bit open. I cupped her cheek, pushing off her hat with the tip of my thumb. It hit the floor behind her.

I backed her against the door, pressing my body to hers, and then lowered my mouth to hers. I kissed her, keeping it light and easy. She let out a breathy sigh and melted into me, her hands fisting the front of my shirt. My stomach clenched with need, but I didn't press too close. I needed to keep my distance for now.

She'd come to me, trusting that I wouldn't be an asshole. And for some strange reason, I didn't want to be one to her. I wanted to be here for her. Give her what she wanted. I broke off the kiss and stepped back, immediately missing the soft curves of her body pressing against mine.

She blinked up at me, her lips slightly moist and swollen, watching as I pulled a piece of paper—a bar receipt—from my pocket and scribbled my name and number on it. "If you wake up and still want to do this? I'll be at the hotel pool at noon. Here's my name and my number, in case you forget it. Meet me down there if you want to continue this without any drinks in your system."

"I'm not drunk," she said. She watched me closely, her brow furrowed. "I'm fine."

I couldn't tell what she was thinking about my refusal to follow her inside her hotel room. She should be grateful I wasn't taking advantage of her drunken state. Lots of other guys would, and then they'd sell the photos they took of her.

"Good." I slipped the piece of paper in her hand before brushing my lips across her forehead. "Then I'll see you tomorrow, won't I? And if you show up, I'll make it worth your time. I promise you that."

I tucked the hat back onto her head, smiling at her one last time before I turned away. She didn't answer me. Just wrapped her arms around herself and watched me leave without blinking. I memorized the way her dress hugged her curves and her long, lean legs that seemed to stretch on for miles, and then…I walked away.

Even though it was the last thing I wanted to do.

CHAPTER *Three*

Mackenzie

The next morning I woke up a little on the late side. Not a huge shocker there, considering the fact that I'd spent most of the night reliving every second I'd spent with Austin, up to the moment when I realized he wasn't going to come inside my room with me. I had to be honest with myself: His refusal had been both a letdown and a turn-on.

It was honorable that he didn't want to take advantage of me, but *man*, I'd wanted to be taken advantage of so freaking bad. I'd been waiting years and years to find the right moment, the right guy. It was really hard to do.

First, there was the drummer at the club Heaven—it had been decorated in all blues and whites. There had been private rooms in it, and I remember laying in the fluffy, cotton ball-like bed staring up at the ceiling. It had been gorgeously painted, with white clouds and blue sky behind it, and I'd been so nervous and excited to finally get to experience life. And then he'd told his whole group of friends he was about to bang Mackenzie Forbes, and had tried to catch me on camera. The tabloid had read: "America's Sweetheart Caught Having Sex in Tawdry Club."

Then there had been the hottie at a private party who I'd been sure was a winner. He'd sweet-talked me into thinking he didn't have a clue who I was or what I did for a living. Heck, he acted as if he only liked me for me, and I'd believed him. I'd gone to the bathroom to freshen up, certain I'd finally found the perfect guy, and that's when he'd called the freaking paparazzi. They'd been waiting for me by the time we left the house, arm in arm. The tabloids that time had read: "America's Sweetheart At It Again: All the Naughty Details."

After that, I'd understandably taken a break from men.

But now I'd finally found a man who fit the bill, and he'd turned me down. Would he be at the pool at noon, or had he been letting me down nicely last night? Heck, the number he'd scribbled down might not even be his. It could be some random number that I'd call and they'd be all, "You totally got dissed at the bar last night, didn't you?"

Maybe that would be all over the tabloids, too. I could see it now: "America's Sweetheart Gets Dissed: Details Inside!"

I rolled over and checked my phone. I had texts from Cassie and Quinn. I shot them both a few replies, spending some time getting caught up on their plans for the day. Quinn was spending the day with some rich boy she'd met the other night, and Cassie was sightseeing. A part of me wanted to go with Cassie and say "screw it" to this whole "getting laid" plan.

But that would be breaking our pact.

We'd gotten separate rooms and vowed to spend as much time as possible trying to live life to its fullest, while also trying our best to have some spring flings in the process. And that meant not hanging out with my girls for once, no matter how hard that was.

I jotted off a last text to Cassie. *Going to get ready for the day. I'll let you know how it goes.*

Barely a second passed before Cassie replied. *All right! Have fun and be safe.*

I dropped the phone to the side and gazed at the clock. It was time to go find my man. I swung my legs over the side of the bed and trotted over to the mirror to eye my reflection. Green eyes and disheveled brown hair stared back at me. I tugged on a strand of hair and bit my lower lip. The dark brown hair had been a big change for me, but I thought it might help me blend in.

It seemed to be working. Austin hadn't recognized me.

Funny how something as simple as a different hair color could throw off a person's perspective. Well, that and I wasn't all made up like I was for videos and awards shows. I looked like a normal woman out to have some fun. It was so refreshing to feel and act normal. To blend into a crowd and have no one notice me.

That's something normal people took for granted. Not that I was complaining or anything. Far from it. I loved my life, and I was blessed to have so many wonderful fans. But sometimes... Sometimes I just wanted to be a twenty-one-year-old.

I turned on my heel, went into the bathroom, and hopped in the shower. After a quick shave and some much-needed moisturizing, I slipped into my tiny bikini, threw on a sarong, and fluffed my wet hair with my fingers. I could blow-dry it, but what was the point? If we ended up actually swimming, it would only get wet anyway.

I slipped into a pair of wedges and left the room, my heart racing the whole time. Would he be there? I had no idea, but I was about to find out.

The elevator doors opened, and I stepped on. It stopped on the floor below mine, and for a second I thought maybe Cassie would step on. They'd let me pay for their vacation, but they'd refused to take a penthouse suite, and this was her floor. If she came onto the elevator with me, I'd take it as a sign that I should hang with her today. Stick with the known rather than venturing into the unknown.

But instead, a small family stepped onto the elevator. Looks like I had to stick with the unknown after all. *Austin, here I come.* My heart raced at the mere thought.

Seeking a distraction, I looked down at the young girl at my side and smiled at her, wiggling my fingers in a small wave. She was already watching me, her eyes narrowed. I held my breath, waiting to see if my cover was blown. I never denied a fan an autograph or a photo, and I wasn't about to start with a girl this young, no matter how badly I wanted my privacy. That wasn't me.

After a couple of seconds, she shook her head and looked away without a squeal. I let out the breath I'd been holding and leaned against the elevator wall, wishing I could tell her she was right about me, without letting the rest of the world know. The remainder of the ride passed quickly, and as I left the elevator I slammed my hat down on my head and headed for the pool, my legs shaky and my palms sweaty.

Would he be there? God, I hoped so.

I walked out in to the sun, scanning the people surrounding the pool. I caught sight of Cassie, but I didn't head over to her, despite my inclination to do so. I had to see if Austin was here. I'd come this far; I wasn't backing down now. After a cursory glance across the crowded pool area, I almost started her way since I didn't see him, but then…

I did. I saw him.

He reclined on the opposite side of the pool from Cassie, an empty lounge chair next to him. He'd set his shirt on the chair next to it, presumably saving it for me. Two girls chatted him up, flirting with him. He replied, but he looked almost bored. Definitely uninterested, if nothing else.

Tattoos covered his chest, and a couple extended to his hard abs, making me stand there motionless, staring like an idiot. I mean, God. He was *hot*. His brown hair was spiked, but it looked natural as opposed to gelled down, and he wore a pair of black swim trunks. Oh, and he also had a six-pack—or maybe there was more than six, geez.

In his hand he held a pair of shades, but he'd taken them off to chat with the girls who were obviously trying to gain his attention. His gaze scanned the entrance, and then fell on me. Even from this distance, I saw his bright blue eyes light up. He shifted his weight, straightening his spine, and then turned his attention back to the girls.

He said a few words, pointed in my direction, and shook his head. The girls turned my way, gave me a dirty look, and huffed away. I took a steadying breath, locked eyes with him, and made my way to his side. The closer I got, the faster my heart beat.

This was it. This was *him*. The guy I'd been waiting for all this time.

It was time to collect.

"Hey," I said, trying to sound casual. "You came."

He removed his shirt from the chair next to him and cocked a brow at me. "Did you doubt I would?"

"Maybe a little bit." I sat down, my gaze dipping to his chest. He had a foreign word across his chest, in Greek lettering, and black tribal tattoos swirled around the word. Flames licked out from the black lines, making the word inside of the design pop. I wondered what that one word meant, but I didn't ask. "Nice ink."

"Thanks." He reclined and crossed his hands behind his head. "Why did you think I wouldn't come? *I* asked *you* to come here with me, not the other way around."

"I didn't think you wouldn't show up," I argued, taking off my sarong and stretching out beside him. I turned my head his way. He was watching me with hooded eyes, and I swore I could feel his gaze on me. How cliché was that? I fisted my hands as my stomach twisted with desire. "I just wasn't sure you would."

He slowly lifted his gaze from my body and met my eyes. "There's a difference?"

"Yeah, there's a difference all right."

He sat up and flipped his legs over the side of the chair. Reaching out, he trailed a finger over my stomach, right above the top of my pink bikini bottoms. "I wouldn't have missed this for the world. I told you I wanted you last night. I just wanted to make sure you really wanted me, and that it wasn't the booze talking."

I sucked in a shaky breath when his hand crept higher, dangerously close to the undersides of my breasts. He kept it strictly PG, but it felt more R because he drove me crazy with need. "I still want you."

"Good." He skimmed over my ribcage, his knuckles scraping my bare skin. All around us, people laughed and chatted and walked, but they all kind of faded away. "I see the big hat's back."

"Yeah." I tugged it lower. "What can I say? I'm a girl who likes her privacy, almost as much as she likes you. I couldn't stop thinking about you last night."

Maybe I should tell him who I was, so he would get why I was hiding from the world. Come clean. But what if he wasn't trustworthy? What if he turned it around on me, and took some pictures to sell to the paparazzi? My agent would throw a freaking fit if that happened again.

His hand brushed across my ribcage, sending shocks of need and desire through me. "You were on my mind, too. All night long. You know, I'd like to get to know you a little bit better. Ask you a few questions, maybe."

I watched his fingers as they crept lower, still remaining perfectly family appropriate…not that there were a whole lot of families here or anything. "Like…?"

"What's your favorite color?"

I laughed lightly. "Easy." I pointed to my bikini. "Light pink. Yours?"

"Green." He cocked his head, his palm splayed across my stomach. It felt…territorial. And I liked it. "Favorite food?"

"Steak. You?"

He slid his hand a tiny bit lower. "Pizza. Always pizza."

"Favorite sport?" I threw in, beating him to the punch.

"Football." He snorted. "Is there any other kind?"

"Same here. Cowboys all the way."

"Blech." He rolled his eyes. "Redskins fan here."

"Washington?" I blinked at him. "Why?"

He looked away, then looked back at me with hard eyes. I had a feeling he hadn't meant to admit that. The man liked his secrets almost as much as I did. "I used to live there when I was a baby. It's where my mom's from, but we moved down here when I was three."

"Oh. Wow. That must have been a big change."

"I don't remember," he answered dismissively. He leaned in, his hand skimming over my hip and slipping almost underneath my butt. "Let's make this more interesting. Favorite position?"

I hesitated, not sure what he was asking me. "You mean in football? I mean, I don't play, but I guess quarterback."

His eyes widened, and then he laughed, throwing his head back. It was the first time I heard him *really* laugh, and it was as musical as his voice. I could listen to it all day long. "Yeah. Sure. We could pretend that's what I meant." He chuckled a little bit more. "I used to play quarterback, you know. In high school."

I turned away, my cheeks hot. Only now did I get what he meant—*sex*. "Actually, to answer your question, I like when the man takes control," I said, dropping my voice low. "I like to lose myself in his touch. In his lips…" I trailed off, my attention on his mouth. I could lose myself in those particular lips for as long as he let me, thank you very much. "I like to forget who I am for that short time."

He let out a small groan. "Is that so?"

"Yes. So tell me, Austin. Are you the type of man that can make a girl lose herself?" I asked boldly. I reached out and rested my hand over his racing heart. "Can you make me forget *everything*?"

He swallowed hard, then lowered his head over mine. But before he could kiss me, he stopped, his lips close, but not close enough. He watched me with so much unspoken promise in his eyes that I didn't even know where to begin collecting.

"I can, but not here." He kissed my knuckles, sending a shiver through my whole body, then pressed my hand against the dimple in his chin. Man, I loved that dimple. "Something tells me that a girl who wants her privacy isn't going to want me making her scream out in public."

He was killing me with those lips…but he was right.

I sat up, my legs brushing his as I did so. "Ready to go to my room?"

"Hell yeah, I am." He stood up and offered me his hand. "Let's go."

I knew, just *knew*, that after I had him…I would be irrevocably different.

There was something in the way he made me feel, the way he treated me, that told me he wasn't like any other man. He would be the guy I measured every other guy up against in the future, and they'd all be found lacking. If I was smart, I'd pick a safer bet. A guy who didn't have this effect on me.

"Mackenzie?" he asked, his brow furrowed. "Are you in, or are you out?"

I looked up at him, taking in the muscles and the warm look in his eyes. The way he waited for me, hand extended, never wavering as he let me decide. Who was I kidding? He was one of a kind. I couldn't let him go without spending some time in his arms. That would be foolish.

I slid my hand into his and stood. "I'm *so* in."

CHAPTER *Four*

Austin

I'd seen it back at the pool. Her hesitation. In a way, she would have been smarter to change her mind. To pick some Ivy League kid down for vacation with a squeaky clean record to have a little fun with. One without tattoos or scars. A kid without a dark past or his own secrets to hide. I wouldn't have blamed her in the slightest.

It would have been the right choice.

But then she had gone and placed her hand into mine, and I forgot all about right choices. All I knew was that I was happy she'd picked me. Thrilled she was taking a chance on a guy like me. I knew it couldn't come easy, the amount of trust she had to place in a man to do this. She had no way of knowing if I'd take advantage of her, or if I was a good enough guy to get naked with.

I wasn't. But I wouldn't be using her. I wouldn't be taking

advantage of her. If anything, I'd let her use me. There was something about her that made me want to do the right thing…whatever the hell that was. She would get what she wanted from me, and then she would move on. She'd go back to her fancy little world of A-list outings and awards shows, and I'd catch glimpses of her here and there on the TV. Maybe I'd even buy her album. But I'd never see her again.

I knew it. She knew it.

And we were both okay with that.

The elevator doors opened and I led her inside the small box, my throat going dry. I almost suggested we take the stairs, but I bit back the suggestion. I stole a glance at her as she swiped her card for the penthouse floor. She was all smooth alabaster skin, and I was ink and scars. She spent her days sunning and singing, and I spent mine dealing with…well, my own shit that I didn't want to think about right now. But despite our differences, I was hers for the next few hours.

After a few seconds she turned to me, her green eyes pinning me in place, and a smile playing at those luscious pink lips of hers. She had freckles on her nose. I'd never seen those in any videos. She must hide them with makeup. I had no idea why. They were endearing. The smile faded. "Um, hi." She gave a tiny wave. "So, why are you looking at me like that?"

"Like what?" I asked quickly, not sure what I'd done.

She thought about it. "I don't know. It's almost as if you can't figure me out or something."

I laughed. "That's because I can't. That's not a bad thing. I find you intriguing."

She tapped her fingers on her thigh. She was only wearing a bikini. Her skirt thing she'd been wearing was draped across her arm. "There's nothing to figure out. I'm just a girl."

"And I'm just a guy. Right?"

She nodded. "A special one, but yeah."

Before I could ask her what she meant by that, the elevator dinged. She headed into the hallway and marched up to her door, swiping her keycard through the slot again. I was glad to be the hell out of that box. I scanned the hallway, taking in the layout. There was only one other room up here, and the floor was fucking huge. This was the only hotel I knew of that actually had a penthouse suite, but I'd never been in it. How big was her room, anyway?

I had a feeling it might be bigger than my whole house.

Once the lock flashed green and beeped, I pushed it open for her. With a quick search of the living room area, it was confirmed. It was definitely bigger than my house. After she tossed her key, hat, and skirt on the table by the door, she turned on me, looking nervous.

"Okay." She wrung her hands. "So…there will be some rules."

I shut the door behind me and crossed my arms. "Rules?"

"Yeah." She tilted her chin up. "I've heard horrible stories about people taking pictures and videos without girls knowing, so I have some ground rules. No cameras or phones in the bedroom."

I was impressed she'd thought this through so thoroughly. I held my phone up and tossed it next to hers. "All right. Done."

"Empty your pockets."

I cocked a brow. "Is this your idea of foreplay? If so, you need a few lessons."

"It's just how it has to be." She wrung her hands again and nibbled on her lower lip. "I've seen too many friends get screwed over by guys, so I always play it safe. Something else my daddy taught me before he died."

I wanted to know more, but I already knew enough. I'd Googled it last night. He'd been killed in a car accident a couple of years ago. Mackenzie was alone now. I knew how that felt all too well, in some ways. "He taught you to strip search men before sex? That was quite the liberal father you had."

"No." She gave me a small smile. "But he taught me to always be smart and never get caught in compromising situations. It's a lesson I'll never forget."

"Fair enough." I emptied my pockets, turning them inside

out to show her I wasn't hiding anything. I couldn't help but be grateful I hadn't shoved much in my swim trunks. Just my keys, phone, and some cash. "See? All gone."

She nodded. "Thank you for your understanding. Now follow me."

"As you wish, milady," I said, bowing to her playfully. "I'm at your service."

She shot me a weird look and I laughed. She was so delightfully paranoid that it was cute. I got that she wanted to be in control of the situation. I even understood it, considering her position in life. For now, I would let her have her way. I would let her boss me around. But once we were behind closed doors, *I* would be the one in control.

After all, it's how she liked it. She'd told me as much.

She led me in to the bedroom, motioning me inside. Then she shut the door behind her and leaned against it, her cheeks pink. She gripped the knob behind her, seeming torn. "There's something you should know. I'm...I'm a..."

I didn't want her to tell me who she was. She didn't need to tell me a thing about herself, because I didn't plan on telling her anything about me. Fair was fair. I cupped her cheek, meeting her eyes. "I don't need to know whatever it is you're afraid to say. All I need to know is where you keep the condoms, because I've got empty pockets."

Her lips twitched into a small smile. "I bought a few boxes and put them by the bed." Her hand lifted then fell, and her cheeks went even redder. "I wasn't sure what type you'd prefer..."

I smiled and backed her toward the bed. If I didn't know better, I'd think she had never done this before, but I knew otherwise. She'd been found with a guy a few months ago, naked and in the throes of passion inside some club. I'd read the story. She was no young miss who hadn't seen a man naked.

Maybe she was just nervous. I could fix that. I tipped her head back with my thumbs under her chin. "Mackenzie?"

"Yeah?" she breathed, her voice soft.

"Close your eyes. Let me take control."

She swallowed hard and did as I asked, her hands balled into tight little fists. "Okay. What now?"

I looked at her for a second, simply enjoying her beauty. Then I did what I'd been dying to do ever since I walked away last night. I kissed her, and this time I didn't hold myself back. As soon as our lips met, I slipped my tongue inside her mouth and pressed her back against the bed.

We fell on to it, her arms tight around me, and I deepened the kiss. Her tongue touched mine, hesitantly at first, but then she groaned and swirled it around mine. She tasted so fucking good. I'd kissed plenty of girls. I'd had plenty of spring break flings. But this? This one girl?

She felt different.

And it wasn't because she was famous. Hell, I didn't give a shit about that. If anything, it made me want to avoid her. The attention being at her side could bring to me wasn't welcome. I had lots of reasons to avoid cameras, lots of darkness in my past that I didn't want shared with the world, but I didn't want to avoid her. I don't think I could have even if I knew it would end badly.

Her nails dug into the back of my neck, stinging, and she wrapped her legs around my waist. There was no more hesitance or nervousness.

There was just *us*.

Mackenzie

Holy crap.

This was what I'd been waiting for all this time. Austin was the man I'd needed all along to be my first. I'd never felt this way. I'd never felt so irreparably turned on and needy and hungry all at once. He pulled me closer to his erection, pressing against me where I ached for his touch.

And oh my God, what an erection it was. I could feel

his hard length against me, burning me through the flimsy bikini I'd worn for him. I rolled my hips against him, my body quivering at the pleasure the motion shot through me.

He broke off the kiss, his lips moving down my jaw and over my shoulder blade. I moaned and arched my neck, granting him better access. Anything to make him keep going. I wanted to feel his lips all over my skin, burning through me. Claiming me. His hand skimmed down my thigh, then crept up the inside.

I had a feeling that this could be more than sex, if either of us allowed it to be. The hold he had over me was strong. Stronger than I'd expected or even thought was possible. "Austin…" I breathed. I didn't even recognize my own voice. "Please. I need you."

"Are you sure you want this?" he asked, his lips pressed to my pulse. "Tell me to stop now if you're not."

I buried my hands in his hair and yanked his head back up to mine. "Yes, I'm sure. Just *do* it already."

His mouth smashed down on mine, claiming me without another word. His fingers brushed over my core, and even through the fabric I could feel his touch searing me. When he brushed against my clit, his finger moving in a circular motion, I whimpered in to his mouth and skimmed my fingers down his back. I curved my hands around his butt, holding him in place.

He wasn't going anywhere.

His other hand cupped my breast, squeezing the aching nipple as he moved his fingers over me. I was strung so tightly I knew, I just knew, I could come with only a few more touches from him. I could feel myself tightening and growing more and more desperate for what he could give me. I arched my back. "*Austin.*"

He slid his fingers inside the bikini bottoms, his mouth moving over mine insistently as his finger traced my opening. "You're so fucking hot," he said, his voice gruff. "So fucking perfect."

"M-More," I begged, my legs opening even wider. "God, I need more."

He grunted and rubbed his thumb over me, fast and hard. I cried out and raked my nails over his back, my head tossing back and forth as the pleasure crashed over me, taking me higher and higher until I wasn't even sure if I was still on this planet. My stomach tightened, and my legs shook and then...

Oh my God, then it all came apart with startling intensity. I let out a cry that sounded half prayer and half plea, clinging to him and burying my face in his shoulder. His fingers froze over me, applying a slight pressure, and I let out a choked sigh.

So *that* was an orgasm. Holy freaking crap.

"Fuck, Mackenzie." He moved lower down my body, kissing his way down my shoulder and toward my breasts. "That was hot."

I let out a sound of agreement, my whole body feeling completely limp from the orgasm he'd just given me...and yet somehow, still wanting more. I might not have firsthand experience, but I knew what I wanted. And it involved his swim trunks going away.

I grabbed a hold of them and yanked. "Lose these."

He nipped at the top of my breast and pushed off the bed with one smooth motion. Geez, everything he did was so freaking hot and sexy and he wasn't even trying. His hands hovered at the waistband, and he ran his gaze up my body. He looked so irresistible, standing there staring at me as if I was his reward for good behavior or something. I took a deep breath and memorized the way he looked.

I needed to write a song about this moment.

He stood beside me, his eyes hot and burning.

It filled me with so much—

"If I'm taking mine off, you need to take something off too," he said, interrupting my composing. That's okay. I could do it later. He played with the strings on his trunks. "The top or the bottom. You can pick."

My heart rate increased. Last time I'd tried to do this, I'd been caught naked inside Heaven—oh, the irony of that—with the asshole who'd sold me out. What if Austin didn't like what he saw? What if I wasn't ready? Hell no. I wasn't backing down now. The only way to continue this was to push through without hesitation.

I forced a smile and lifted my hips. "I choose both."

His hands fisted on his trunks. "Do it," he rasped.

I reached down and shimmied out of my bottoms, not letting myself hesitate or wimp out. He wanted to see me naked, and I wanted him to see me. It was as simple as that. After I kicked off the bottoms, I reached behind me and undid the strings at my neck, then my back. The whole time I did this, he stood there watching me, his jaw ticking.

I looked at him. Really looked at him. His body was hard and toned and freaking perfect. I'd seen lots of men over the years. Some with six-packs, some with paunchy bellies, and everything in between. But I'd never seen him. His tattoos ran over his pecs and his muscular arms, but I'd already seen that. His brown hair was as soft as it looked—I knew that now—and his blue eyes were hot for me. His bare thighs were rock hard and devoid of any ink, and his erection jutted out from a small patch of curls, begging to be touched and stroked.

"Take it off," he demanded, still holding the waistband of his trunks, probably ready to pull them back up if I didn't follow his instructions. I held the scraps of fabric to my breasts with one hand, the other flailing uselessly at my side. "I need to see you. All of you."

I dropped it. He took a shaky breath, his eyes narrow, and he yanked his trunks the rest of the way off. He was naked. Perfectly, startlingly *naked*. "Fuck. Who knew America's Sweetheart was hiding the body of a pinup model under those cute dresses?"

I stiffened. "What did you just call me?"

"Huh?" He climbed onto the bed, his eyes latched with mine. Then he stopped, his own going wide. "Mackenzie…"

"You know? Oh my God. No, no, no." I scrambled away

from him, ripping the robe off the chair by my bed. I shrugged into it and hugged it tight, searching the room for cameras. But then I remembered there couldn't be any. He'd taken everything out of his pockets. I squeezed my eyes shut, closing out the world—and him, too. "God, not again."

I couldn't be betrayed again. Couldn't see it blasted all over the tabloids again.

Finally, I opened my eyes and looked at him. He sat there, naked in the middle of my bed, looking perfectly calm about it, and lifted a hand. "Mackenzie, calm down. This isn't what it looks like."

What would the headline read now? Probably: America's Sweetheart Is An Idiot! That's what it should say, because once again, a guy who I was trying to get intimate with had lied to me. Maybe I was destined to be single and alone, and I just had to accept that. "How long have you known?"

He flinched. "Since the second you took off your hat."

"Of course you did," I said woodenly. I'd never learn my lesson, would I? "I should call the cops on you right now."

He stiffened. "I didn't do anything wrong, so calling the cops is a waste of time."

"You know who I am," I accused. "But you didn't tell me."

He rolled off the opposite side of the bed and sighed. "Yeah, and that's totally a punishable crime. Lock me up for not admitting I knew you were famous."

Well, when he put it that way, of course it sounded stupid. Because it was. "Why didn't you tell me the truth?"

He put his hands on his hips. He was still naked. "I didn't tell you because you didn't tell me. You obviously didn't want to. Why should I ruin the mood by admitting I knew? What good would it serve?"

"It's called honesty," I snapped. I wanted to believe him, but if he'd been hiding that from me, then what else could he be hiding? For all I knew he was a freaking reporter for TMZ or something. "You should try it sometime."

"Seriously?" He raised a brow. He was so freaking

distracting in his nakedness. I mean, how was I not supposed to look at him? "You're going to preach honesty with me when you hid your identity from me?"

"I did it for a reason," I said, my cheeks heating.

"Maybe I did, too." He picked up his trunks and stepped into them. "Ever think of that? Or do you have to be a celebrity to be entitled to lie?"

He stepped toward me. When I stumbled back from him, my heart racing, he stopped and glowered at me. I flushed at the sign of weakness I'd given him. "Just…stay there. I can't think when you touch me."

He dragged a hand through his hair. "Fine. But knowing who you are doesn't change anything. I'm still here, and I still want you. You can trust me not to tell anyone or sell the story, just like you could have if you never found out I knew who you were."

I shook my head. "I can't trust you anymore. You lied to me."

"Oh, for fuck's sakes," he gritted out. Then he crossed the room and grabbed my arms, his grip firm but not painful. "I'm not going to sell you out, but I'm not going to fucking beg you either. Like I said, in my world, you're in or you're out."

I wanted to be in, but he'd already lied to me once. That was a warning sign if I'd ever seen one. I put a hand to his chest, but didn't shove him away. I could have, but I didn't. "Well, I'm out."

He kissed me hard, his tongue dueling for dominance with mine. By the time he was done, I wasn't sure if I wanted to send him away or throw him back onto my bed. "You know how to find me if you come to your fucking senses. I'd like to finish what we started, but if you refuse to trust me, I can't force you. Believe it or not, I don't usually have to swear to honesty to get in a girl's bed. And I damn well don't have to beg." His fingers smoothed over my skin, and then he let go of me. "Goodbye, Mackenzie Forbes."

He gave me one last heated look and turned on his heel. I

stood there, watching him leave, and bit my lip. Damned if I didn't want to call him back to my room.

But I stayed silent.

CHAPTER

Austin

*L*ater that night, I swiped the rag across the surface of the bar, pressing a little harder than necessary, even though the surface was pretty damn clean already. There were only a handful of locals sitting there, and it had been slow all night. Normally I'd be bummed, but tonight I welcomed it.

Ever since Mackenzie had kicked me out of her room, I'd been in a bad mood.

I tossed the rag over my shoulder and scanned the crowd. At first I passed right over her, completely missing her. But then I caught sight of her oversized hat and I did a double take. Yep, that was definitely her. And she was staring at me.

I wanted to go up to her and ask if she was here to finish what we'd started earlier, but I refused to give in to the urge. She was the one who'd told me to leave, so I had. If she wanted to talk again, she could damn well come up to me. The last hour of my shift passed slowly, and she spent most of it on her phone, her fingers sweeping over the screen without fail.

The rest of the time, she watched me.

I could feel her eyes burning into me as I chatted up the customers and laughed. Every time I talked to one of the female regulars, Mackenzie grew tense and her fingers would hover over the screen instead of touching it. I might not be an expert at relationships and all the shit that came with them, but I was pretty damn positive that she was actually jealous. Of a woman who, more often than not, required help into a cab at the end of the night because she'd be that fucked up.

I wanted Mackenzie and she wanted me. It shouldn't be this complicated.

After I closed out my drawer and slipped my tips in my pocket, I punched out and headed for the door without going over to her. She had to show me a sign. Something besides sitting there pouting at me, for Christ's sakes. I didn't have time for childish games.

I was halfway to the door by the time she must have realized I wasn't coming over to her. She pushed back from the table and came stumbling after me. She had on a pair of "fuck me" heels, a red sundress, and that damn hat.

"Austin, wait," she hissed, tugging her hat lower.

I stopped and turned to her, my brow up. "Can I help you?"

"Stop acting like you don't know it's me," she said. "We both know you do."

"Actually," I crossed my arms, "I can't see your face with that fucking hat on, so how am I supposed to know who you are?"

She ripped it off her head and tossed her hair behind her shoulders. Her eyes were spitting fire at me. "There. Happy?"

"Not really. If you want honesty from me—which you made perfectly clear you do—I'm horny as hell and feeling like an ornery bastard at the moment. I'm off to take care of that particular issue right now."

"Seriously?" she said, her eyes wide. "Just like that, you're

41

moving on?"

Nope. But I certainly wasn't going to let her know she'd gotten under my skin. She didn't need to know I'd be jerking off to the memory of her coming on that damn hotel bed—or that I'd be alone. "I'd prefer you, but well, you made your stance clear on how you feel about me after I let you know I knew who you were. Unless you changed your mind…?" I gave her a few seconds to tell me if she had, since she'd been staring at me for more than an hour, but she didn't say a word. I inclined my head and started for the door again. "All right, then. Enjoy your stay."

"*Wait.*"

I stopped again. "Yes?"

"You lied to me."

I sighed. "We went over this already. I don't get a lot of free time, so I don't want to spend it arguing with you about something we already went over. I didn't lie. I just didn't tell you I knew who you were. There's a difference."

"Is there anything else I need to know about you? Things you're hiding?"

I opened my mouth and then closed it. A million of my secrets came to mind, but they were just that—secrets. "No."

"Are you sure?"

I swallowed hard. "Yep."

"All right." She took a deep breath, her gaze dropping to the floor. "I guess we can go back to my room again."

The way she said it, as if she was bestowing a favor upon me, sat wrong. I knew she didn't mean it that way, but it sounded like it. She might be a superstar and I might be a normal guy, but that didn't mean she was doing me a favor by agreeing to fuck me.

"Why?" I backed her into the corner of the bar, my hands on either side of her head. "Tell me why it has to be me. Why not find another guy?"

Her chin tilted up defiantly. "I don't know. It just does."

"I need a better answer than that." I pressed my hips into

her, letting her feel how hot for her I was. "Why do you want it to be me?"

She blew out a breath. "Because I need you so badly it hurts."

I lowered my head to her neck, kissing the spot where her pulse raced. If she gave me some bullshit answer about choosing me because I was convenient, I would walk away without looking back, no matter how much it hurt my aching cock. "But why do you need it to be *me*?"

"Because I've gotten to kiss you and touch you," she breathed. "And now that I've had a taste of you, no one else will do. It *needs* to be you."

Perfect fucking answer. "Are you sure this time?"

She gripped my work T-shirt with both hands, mangling the bar logo in the upper left corner. "Yes. Please take me home."

I nodded once, then pushed off the wall. "Let's go."

Mackenzie

I hadn't been intending to bring him back to my room, per se. I'd been thinking about sharing a drink or two, talking so we could get to know one another all over again, maybe. I'd told myself to move on and forget about him over and over again, but I couldn't.

There was something about him that wouldn't let me move on. Something that called to me, demanding satisfaction. There was nothing to be done for it. He'd gotten under my skin, and the only way to get him out was to give in to the urge.

To give him another shot.

So...I'd gone to his bar and waited. His whole shift, I'd sat at the table and texted Carrie and Quinn, waiting for him to get off and come over to me. But then he'd started to leave without saying a word, and I'd gone to him instead. I knew I still wanted him. Enough that I was throwing the possible consequences to the floor and stomping on the warning signs written all over this freaking situation.

Even though I'd called my people in Nashville and asked for them to look into him for me, there was no waiting or holding back. Not this time. I might as well have not even bothered to ask. By the time they came back with info on him, I'd probably be home.

I stole a quick glance at him as we entered my hotel lobby. The doorman bowed to me, and I smiled and inclined my head. Austin watched me silently, like he had been since I told him I wanted him and only him. He was treating me the same way he'd treated me before he'd admitted he knew who I was. Like I was just a girl he'd met at a bar. I think that's one of the things I liked most about him.

Sometimes I forgot how the real world worked, and he was so refreshingly real.

I swiped my card to gain access to my floor, and then the elevator doors shut in front of us. "Austin?"

He'd been texting or emailing on his phone, but he shoved it into his pocket and turned to me. "What? Are you having doubts again?" he asked, dragging a hand through his hair.

Heck no. I wanted him.

I shoved him back against the elevator wall. Before he had a chance to so much as blink, I kissed him and pressed my body to his. Ever since I'd sent him away, I'd been burning with the need to finish what we'd started. The mere idea of changing my mind was ludicrous, so I figured the best way to show him how serious I was about doing this was to kiss him. It worked.

His hands cupped my butt, hauling me closer, and he moaned into my mouth. With one whirl, he had me pressed against the wall and his hands were roaming all over my body. My breasts. My hips. My butt. He was everywhere and yet not in enough places.

The elevator beeped and we sprang apart, our breathing heavy. The doors opened and I bolted out of there, Austin hot on my heels. I unlocked the door, took off my hat, and turned on him.

Once he shut the door behind him, I offered a smile and motioned at his pockets. "You know the deal."

He emptied his pockets and followed that up by removing his shirt. I swallowed hard, my eyes feasting on his muscles. God, he looked good and he knew it. Men like him should walk around shirtless all the time. Women would fall at his feet and beg to be his. He could rule the freaking world with a grin and a muscle flex.

I'd be the first to fall.

"I…" I flinched at the way my voice came out all weak and breathy. I didn't do simpering and weak. Time to take control. I walked backward toward the bedroom, gripping the hem of my dress and lifting it slightly. "I want you. In the bedroom we go."

His hands fisted at his sides and he followed me into the room, closing the door securely behind him. His heated gaze dropped down my body. "Take it off."

"This?" I lifted my dress a little higher, but didn't remove it. "Lose the rest of yours first."

He raised his brows. "You bossing me around, sweetheart?"

"And if I am?" I bit down on my lower lip. "You got a problem with that?"

"Hell no. But once we're in that bed, I'm in control." He undid his shorts, but didn't take them off. "I'm just making sure we're clear."

"Crystal." I lifted the dress a little higher. "Now lose the shorts for me."

His lips twitched and he let them hit the floor. All he wore was a pair of skintight green boxer briefs. Oh my God, I could write countless songs about that body of his.

Heck, about *him* in general.

His shoulders were toned to perfection, tapering down to his thin waist and straight hips, showing me just how in shape he was. Every line, crease, and muscle was chiseled as if it was done by hand. He watched me with an undeniable hunger in

45

his blue eyes, his dimple more pronounced with the way he'd squared off his jaw.

And the way his boxer briefs hugged the bulge of his erection? Holy hell, I could write a song about that, too. Freaking perfect. He was beautiful.

Sucking in a deep breath, I lifted my dress over my head and tossed it onto the floor. When I stood in front of him— wearing nothing but a pair of heels, a thong, and a black bra—I placed my hands on his shoulders and slowly trailed my nails down his chest, over his abs, and then stopped at the waistband of his boxers.

I wanted to do so many things to him right now. Touch him in so many ways. But I dropped to my knees and tugged his boxers down, freeing his erection. His hands threaded into my hair and he tensed, looking down at me with blazing eyes. "Mackenzie?"

I tipped my head back and looked up at him. "Yeah?"

"You don't have to…" He gestured down. "Let me get you in bed."

I shook my head. "Not yet." Without dropping my gaze, I flicked my tongue over the tip of his shaft. "I'm not ready."

And then I closed my mouth around him, sucking gently.

His abs jerked in response, and his hands tightened on my hair. His blue eyes blazed down at me; so hot and intoxicating I couldn't look away until he closed his lids, hiding them from me. "Holy shit."

I sucked him in deeper, swirling my tongue over him as I did so. His entire body went tense, and he gripped my hair so tight it stung. I could tell he was making himself hold still for me. Forcing himself not to move or so much as flinch. But when I pulled back, releasing him from my mouth, he groaned and pushed back inside, his corded muscles flexing as he did so.

It was the most erotic thing I'd ever seen or done.

A pang of need shot my stomach, and I let my lids drift shut. As I took him deeper inside of me, sucking a little harder,

I cupped his butt in my hands, holding him where I wanted him. He groaned and thrust closer, gently yet insistently. I swirled my tongue over him again, digging my nails into his skin.

"Fuck," he gasped. His face red, he pulled me off him and tossed me back on the bed. I hit it full force, bouncing slightly. Before I settled back on to the mattress, he was on top of me, pressing his glorious length to my core. "My turn to play," he growled.

He ripped off my bra as his mouth crashed down on mine, and I trembled from the force of the desire that tore through me. He kept kissing me all over, intoxicating me, as he slid down my body. He grabbed one of my ankles, and his mouth left mine. He removed my shoes, one by one, then kissed the spot right next to my knee.

Holy freaking crap that felt *good*.

It felt even better when his hands skimmed up my inner thighs, and he followed them with his lips. He gripped my underwear, tugging them lower, even as he moved his kisses higher. By the time I was naked, I was already halfway to an orgasm, and he'd barely even touched me.

My reaction to him was off the charts. Ridiculous is what it was.

And oh-so-delicious.

He knelt between my legs, lifting my hips higher. I knew what he was about to do, and I tensed in anticipation. I'd had it done to me once before, at Heaven when I'd been caught naked, and it had been okay—even without the orgasm. I had a feeling that with Austin it would be more than okay.

And boy, I was right.

The second his tongue touched me, my entire body quivered with pleasure and need and something I couldn't quite describe. Almost a too-intense feeling that threatened to take me over if I let it. And I wanted it to, because it felt that good.

I arched my back, giving myself over to him, and he

rolled his tongue over me again, his hands gripping my butt and holding me in place. This was what I'd been missing out on. This is what I wanted. *Him.* I latched on to the pleasure spreading through my veins. My stomach tensed, squeezing so tight I could barely breathe. Just when I was sure I would never catch my breath again, something snapped inside me, sending me spiraling over the edge.

Another mind-blowing orgasm, of course.

He let me fall back down on the mattress and shoved off the bed, stalking to where I'd told him I had the condoms. He ripped the drawer open, grabbed one, and opened it. As he rolled it on his erection, he watched me with hooded eyes. The second it was on, he laid on top of me, his lips meeting mine forcefully.

I spread my thighs wider for him, letting him anchor himself inside my legs. When I felt him at my entrance, I tensed, unable to keep myself relaxed. He didn't seem to notice. He kept kissing me, his hands reaching beneath me to tilt my hips upward.

I broke free of the kiss, taking a gasping breath. Maybe I should warn him I was technically still a virgin. Guys could tell that stuff, right? I licked my lips and gripped his shoulders. "I—"

He kissed me again and thrust inside me, hard and sure. I cried out into his mouth, feeling like I'd been ripped in half. He froze, his mouth still on mine but no longer kissing me. Then slowly, oh so slowly, he reared back, his eyes wide and his face pale. "Mackenzie? You are…you were…a…?"

I blinked back tears, biting down on my lip hard and nodding. "Y-Yes."

"Hell. Why didn't you tell me?"

"I was going to. Just now." He started to pull out, but I closed my legs around him and shook my head. "No. Don't go."

"But you're fucking *crying*," he gritted out, his muscles flexing in his arms as he held himself above me. His hard features cracked a little bit. He made a broken sound and

48

kissed me gently. "I'm so sorry I hurt you. I would've been gentler if I knew. I just thought…"

I flinched. "The whole world thought, but they kind of stopped it from happening, ironically enough. I got branded a slut, and I was still a virgin."

He pressed his lips together, his eyes flashing. "You're not a slut, and you're not a virgin anymore." He moved inside me, slow and gentle. He kissed me tenderly, his lips lingering over mine. "How's that feel?" he asked, his voice tense and strained against my mouth.

"Good," I breathed. "Do it again."

He let out a strangled moan and moved inside me, in and out, slow and easy. "Fuck, you feel good. Too good." Sweat broke out on his forehead, and he dropped it to mine. "I don't want to hurt you."

"I know." I closed my eyes and lifted my face to his, wanting another one of his magical kisses. "You won't."

He melded his lips to mine, his tongue slipping easily inside. The pain gave way to the need he brought out in me, and I clung to him, lifting my hips to his when he moved inside me again. Each time he thrust, he went deeper. Harder.

And within mere moments, I was as desperate for him as I'd been before the pain. I raked my nails down his back, begging for more. Needing the release only he could give me, but scared to grab it at the same time. "*Austin*."

He reached between our bodies, pressing his fingers to my clit. "I've got you. Just let go."

I arched my back, pressing closer to him, and the pressure built higher and higher until I knew I was about to crash and burn. He held me close the whole time, saying naughty things as he moved inside me. The tightly wound string snapped, and I came, stars bursting in my vision.

My entire body went limp, and he thrust one last time, his body stiffening. He collapsed on top of me, burying his face in my neck and whispering, "Mackenzie."

I closed my eyes and held him close, my racing heart

gradually slowing to normal speeds. By the time he lifted his head and looked at me, I was almost ready to come back down to earth…even if I didn't want to.

CHAPTER

Austin

My arms tightened around her, not wanting to let go. My mind was reeling over the fact that she'd been a fucking virgin, of all things. How could Mackenzie Forbes have spent the last, I don't know, five years a virgin? Hell, I'd lost my own innocence at fifteen and I hadn't been in the spotlight.

Maybe that's what had held her back. The scrutiny.

For the first time in my life, I had questions about a girl I'd spent a handful of hours in bed with. For the first time in my life, I needed to know more. I wasn't sure what to do with that, so I went with it. I opened my fucking mouth. "Mackenzie…?"

"Yeah?" she asked, her voice dreamy.

I lifted up on my elbows, my eyes searching hers. She nibbled on her lower lip. "So, uh, the paparazzi strikes again with their lies? There were all those stories about you…"

She huffed out a breath. "Yeah, they were obviously lies," she drawled, her Southern twang a little more pronounced than before. "Except the one where I was found in that club. That was real, but they kind of interrupted us. The rest was pure fiction."

I shook my head. "Unbelievable. Can't you do something about that? Sue them for libel or something? That doesn't seem like it's legal."

"I could, but why bother? They'd just come up with more stories. It's a never-ending fight. One I don't have the time or energy to deal with."

She might not have the energy to deal with it, but *I* did. And I wanted to bash their fucking skulls together for making up lies about her. "But—"

She covered my mouth with two fingers. "It is what it is. It's how the world works."

"The hell it is," I growled. "Let me spend a few minutes with the dickheads making this shit up and I'll get them to stop."

Her lips twitched, and she smiled up at me. "It's sweet of you to offer, but no thanks. You can't win. Everyone loves to see how messed up people like me are." She lifted a shoulder and the smile faded away. "Even if it's not exactly true."

I kissed her forehead and hugged her close, a surge of protectiveness coming over me. I couldn't help it. I kind of had a knight-in-shining-armor complex going on. I tried to fight it, but it wouldn't go the fuck away. Knights were tricky like that. "I'm sorry."

"Thanks." She let out a half snort-half laugh. "But it's hardly a tragedy. So people think I'm a little slutty while I'm really a virgin? There are worse things in the world. Poverty. Sickness. Death. I hardly have room to complain, ya know?"

Well, she had a point. But it still sucked. "For what it's worth…I'm glad you chose me for this, uh, thing."

"Why?" Her brow rose, and the solemnity left her eyes. She trailed her fingers over my chest, making me suck in a deep breath. Already, I wanted her again. What the fuck was up with that? "You got a thing for virgins, Austin?"

I snorted. "I wouldn't know. You were my first one."

"Not even your first time?"

"Nope. She was my tutor, and a grade above me. Let's just say…she taught me more than math." I grinned. "Much more."

She rolled her eyes. "Why am I not surprised by this information?"

"Hey, what can I say? I was irresistible even back then."

"Oh God." She swatted my arm. "Get off me, you big oaf."

Laughing, I rolled to the side and watched her climb out of bed. She quickly wrapped herself in her silk robe, her cheeks pink. She was still embarrassed by her nudity. How refreshingly charming. Most of the women I spent time with walked around naked more than they did clothed.

"Do you have security here?"

She shook her head. "I didn't let them come. I wanted to be normal for a little while."

"What about at school?"

She scrunched her nose. "Yeah, but only one. It's more of a precautionary measure. Most of the people there don't give a damn who I am. There's been a few pictures here and there of me, but not much. I keep to myself." She paused. "Well, me, Quinn, and Cassie do."

I had the feeling they were very close, those three girls. Which made me wonder… "Why aren't they in the same room as you?"

"We all wanted to be free to bring guys home. It's kinda hard to do if you're sharing rooms."

I laughed. "You have a point. Are they up here, too?"

"Nope, they're a floor lower, in separate rooms. They wouldn't let me book the penthouse for them. That's where they drew the line when it came to me paying for them, but it worked out. There's only one more up here as it is."

"Wait." I sat up straight. "You paid for them to come here?"

"Yeah, of course." She looked at me, her forehead creased.

"Why wouldn't I? I can certainly afford it, and they're my best friends."

Respect swept over me, even more so than before. She was so damn generous and didn't even realize it. "Why did you come here, of all places, and not somewhere less crowded? Aren't you worried you'll be spotted?"

"I was hoping to blend in with the crowd since it's so crazy. It's worked so far. Between the darker hair and no makeup, I'm just another girl."

When she turned back to me, her dark hair framing her face, I almost forgot to breathe. She was so fucking gorgeous. So fucking different. "Speaking of which, I love those freckles you hide in your videos. They're adorable, like you. You're beautiful."

Where had that sappy statement come from? Must be that damn knight again…

"Uh, thanks." Her wide eyes met mine, and her cheeks flushed even more. She tucked a stray piece of hair behind her ear. "So are you."

No one had ever called me beautiful before. It made something inside me shift or stop blocking the way to my heart. I didn't like that. "Thanks, I think."

"Why do you *think* you thank me?"

"I've never been called beautiful before. Hot. Sexy. Fuckable." I shrugged. "Sure. Lots of times. But never beautiful. It doesn't seem to fit me."

"Well…" She bit down on her lower lip. "I think it fits perfectly."

A fist punched my chest. I'd swear it had. I opened my mouth to scoff at her reply, or to retort I was scarred, broken, and ugly. But nothing came out. I didn't want to argue with her. If she thought I was beautiful, maybe that was a good thing. So I didn't say a word. Just stared at her, speechless for the first time in my fucking life.

"So, uh, now what?" She shifted her weight and wrung her hands in front of her. "I'm obviously not accustomed to what happens next, since I never got this far before."

There it was again. That adorable innocence she had going on. It was irresistible to a messed-up guy like me. I smiled and stole a quick glance at the clock. I had another hour before I had to be home. "What do you want to happen?" I asked softly.

"I…" She bit down harder on her lip. "If you'd like to, I'd like to spend the rest of my time here with you. When you're free, of course. I know you have a job and everything. Unless you're a one-time guy. That's fine, too."

"You're not going to be with your friends?"

She shook her head. "They're off having their own adventures. It's all part of the plan—get laid and have fun. They need it as much as I do."

"Ah, gotcha," I said, rubbing my jaw and hiding the grin that inexplicably formed. "You're doing pretty good in your portion of the plan."

She blushed again. I fucking loved that blush. "I'd say so. I have you." She rested her hands on my chest, raising those bright green eyes to mine. "So, are you interested in hanging out a bit more?"

I did the math. Four more days with her? It wasn't a hard decision to make. "I'm in. If I'm not working, I'm yours. How's that sound?"

"Perfect." She let go of me and backed up. Then she wrapped her arms around herself and looked toward the window. Her profile was so fucking perfect it stole my breath away. "We need to set some ground rules, though."

I flopped down on the bed again and reclined against the headboard, crossing my arms behind my neck. Man, she liked her fucking rules almost as much as I liked her. "No pictures. No selling you out. No feelings. No attachments. Just fun, no-strings-attached sex?"

She blinked at me. "Yeah. Pretty much. I'll be leaving and—"

"And I'll be staying." I raised a brow. "I am well aware of this fact, seeing as I, you know, *live* here and all. Has anyone ever told you that you have the tendency to point out the obvious?"

She put her hands on her hips. "Yeah, maybe."

"Well, you should work on that. I thought you were flawless, now I find I'm wrong? It breaks my heart."

She shook her head, but her lips twitched into a small smile. "I don't want anyone to get hurt. Is that so wrong?"

I reached out and snatched her by the hips, pulling her back in to the bed with me. "What makes you so sure I'll be the one who gets hurt? Maybe you'll be the one who won't want to leave me, and I'll have to be all—" I held a hand to my heart and tried my best to look brokenhearted. I'd never suffered from that affliction before, so I might have failed. "'Babe, you need to get on with your life. Do a few tours. Sing a few songs. Then you'll forget all about me. I promise.'"

She laughed. "Oh my God. Has anyone ever told you that you're incorr—"

I kissed her into silence. I'd always wanted to do that to a girl, but never stuck around long enough to get to that point. I was more of a take-em-and-leave-em type of guy, and I made sure the girls I took and left were the same way.

Hell, Mackenzie was even one of those girls. She just wanted some no-strings-attached fun, and I was the perfect guy for that, since it's all I did. I hugged her closer, my hands tightening on her without conscious thought. Her arms snaked around my neck, holding me tight. It felt like it was meant to be or some other corny-ass thought.

I conveniently ignored my sappy side and smiled against her lips before breaking off the kiss. "It worked."

"What did?" she asked distractedly, her hands playing with my hair.

"Kissing you into silence. I always see people do it in movies, and I thought it was pure bullshit." I kissed her again. Light. Fleeting. "Now I know it's not."

"You've never kissed someone to shut them up before?" she asked, watching me with those intense green eyes. How many videos of hers had I seen where they zoomed in to her face and her heavily made-up eyes? I liked her better like this. Natural and real. "I'd have thought you did it to dozens of women already."

She thought I was a man-whore? I didn't know how I felt about that. Sure, I didn't take things seriously when it came to women, and I didn't do relationships, but I wasn't exactly fucking all the women in Florida. I shrugged. "I'm kind of like you in that respect. I never let anyone get too close."

"Hm." She pressed a finger against my chin, then kissed my dimple. The sweet gesture did foreign things to my heart. "Why not?"

She made me want to tell her, which was all the more reason for me not to. I shook my head, then bumped the tip of her nose with my finger. "If I told you, I'd be letting you close."

"Is that such a bad thing?"

"Yep." I rolled her underneath me, settling between her thighs. "We're easy and light, right? No feelings. No whispered confessions. And for my part, I promise not to fuck you over."

The last time I'd uttered those words had been after I failed big time. I wouldn't fail again. This time, I was sure of my success. I wouldn't sell her out.

"I know you won't." She pursed her lips. "It's why I picked you."

"You thought I looked trustworthy?" I looked down at myself. First, she'd called me beautiful, and now she seemed to think she could believe in me. I was starting to wonder if she needed glasses. Had she even looked at me at all? I was beginning to doubt it. "It's the tats, isn't it? They just scream of reliability."

She shrugged. "You might try to look like a bad boy, but I don't think you are."

I reared back. "Hold on a second—"

"No." She grabbed my arms, holding me in place. I could have broken the hold, but I didn't. "You looked like the kind of guy who would understand me. I have a feeling you've been pushing people away since you were old enough to let someone in. Maybe something happened to you that changed you? Defined who you were. Whatever it was, it made you closed off. Maybe it was something to do with your parents…"

My heart faltered. She was way too close to the truth with that one. "It's spring break. You need to stop analyzing me like I'm an assignment." I rolled her onto her back and pushed off the bed. "And with that? I gotta go."

"I'm sorry. I didn't mean to analyze you."

I pulled on my boxers. "It's fine. And I'm not leaving because of your questions." I stepped into my pants, not quite meeting her eyes. "I've got something I have to do, but I'm free all day tomorrow. Want to hang out? I can plan a day of fun and relaxation. Maybe some snorkeling?"

"I'd love to spend the day with you, and snorkeling sounds perfect." She hesitated. "We just have to keep it private. Nothing too public where people might recognize me."

I looked at her, regretting my decision to leave already. She looked so damn kissable laying there, freshly fucked. "I know. You trust me, right?"

She looked down at her hands, which were clenched in her lap. "Yeah. Of course."

"Good." Satisfaction hit me deep, and I tilted her chin up so I could drop a quick kiss on her lips. For some reason her trust was important to me. "I'll come pick you up at nine in the morning. Wear a bathing suit with a dress or shorts. Okay?"

"Yeah, that sounds—" She cut herself off and held up a hand. "Oh, wait. I have breakfast with the girls in the morning, so we can catch up on our escapades so far. Can we make it ten?"

"Sure."

I kissed her one last time, grabbed my shirt off the floor, and walked out of the room. As I shoved my keys into my pocket, I took a steadying breath. Walking out into the hallway, I checked my texts.

I had a few from my buddy Chris and one from Rachel.

My role in her life was the thing I wasn't willing to share with anyone...not even Mackenzie. Some things were better left unexplained. I dialed her number and lifted my phone to my ear. She picked up right away. "Austin? Where the heck are you?"

"I'm on my way home."

"Can you bring pizza?" She turned the music down, then I heard her flop down on her bed. Ironically enough, she was listening to Mackenzie. Not a huge surprise there. She was always listening to Mackenzie. "I'm freaking starving."

"Depends. Did you clean your room like I asked you to?"

She sighed. "Yep. I even folded my laundry without you asking."

"Hm." I pushed the button on the elevator, smoothing my hand over my tousled hair. I swore I could still feel Mackenzie's fingers running through it. "I guess that constitutes a reward. Pick your topping, sis."

She closed a book. She was almost always buried in a book. "I'll call it in, and you can pick it up on the way home."

I smiled and stepped onto the elevator. She sounded so much older than her sixteen years sometimes. Of course, with a dad like ours, how could she not have grown up faster? The smile faded from my lips at the mere memory of that asshat. "Deal. I'll be home in twenty."

"See you then, bro."

"Bye, squirt."

"Austin," she admonished. "I told you to stop calling me that when I turned fourteen. You need to respect my request."

Then she hung up on me.

I laughed and dropped my phone into my pocket, staring at the numbers as I climbed lower and lower. It was weird that I'd just come from Mackenzie Forbes's hotel room, and I couldn't even tell anyone. It was a secret, and I got that. But Rachel would fucking flip out if she ever got to meet Mackenzie.

The thought of the joy it would bring to her almost made me want to ask Mackenzie for the favor. Rachel never had much of a reason to smile. I would do anything to make her smile like she used to, before Dad ruined it all.

Before he ruined us both.

I'd been twenty-two. She'd been fourteen.

They'd tried to place her in a home after my dad went all crazy, but I'd insisted on taking her myself. I'd already let her down once, and I wouldn't do it again. Even after two years of her living with me, I still had visits from social workers on a monthly basis. No one thought I could handle her.

They underestimated how much I loved her.

I wouldn't let her down again. She was my fucking world, and always would be. I'd been busting my ass to keep a roof over her head and food on the table ever since I took over her guardianship. I even had a small college fund for her, because there was no doubt in my mind she'd be going. She was a smart kid.

The elevator doors opened. I stepped out of them, then headed out into the hot Key West night. I loved it here. Loved the heat and the energy and the music. But sometimes I wished I could pack up Rachel and run away. Go somewhere else. But where would we go? She'd lived here her whole life, and it felt wrong ripping her away from what she knew. Part of me thought it would be a good thing. A fresh start of sorts. Maybe it would help her forget.

But nothing could erase bad memories. I knew that all too fucking well.

God knows I'd tried.

CHAPTER *Seven*

Mackenzie

The next morning, I leaned back in my chair and looked at my breakfast companions, Quinn and Cassie. They were watching me intently, waiting for me to tell them more about Austin. They didn't trust him. I could tell by the way they kept sharing long, lingering looks. But I did trust him.

I didn't know why I did, but it was true.

Sighing, I continued. "You guys worry too much. I was only saying that I knew he was hiding something from me."

Cassie nodded. "But that's reason to worry, right?"

"What do you know about him?" Quinn asked, sipping her drink.

I played with my cup of tea. "He's a bartender who sings for fun and doesn't want to be in the spotlight. And he has tattoos. Oh, and he's a great kisser…among other things." I grinned when they made little cheering sounds. "I had my people look into him, but there's no reply yet."

"Well, now that you got what you wanted from him, maybe you should take a step back," Quinn said. "You know. Distance yourself from him a little bit."

"I agree. He might be hiding something big," Cassie muttered, peeking over her shoulder and playing with her blonde hair. "Maybe he's a creep or something."

"Um…" I blinked at her, squinting at her tired appearance. Cassie had dark circles under her gray eyes, almost as if she'd been busy getting some action last night, but I knew better. She hadn't been. Her texts had been filled with frustration over the guy she'd fallen for—the guy who had a girl waiting for him back home. "He's not a creep. He's a good guy. I would know it if he wasn't."

Quinn rolled her eyes at Cassie's comment. Quinn, on the other hand, looked refreshed and quite satisfied, as she should. She'd been getting it on all vacation, and looked all the better for it. "Not everyone is a psycho, Cass." Quinn looked at me. "She's been super paranoid lately. You'd think she saw a dead body or something."

Cassie paled. "Being careful isn't a stupid idea. We don't know any of these guys we're hanging out with."

"Tell me more about your off-limits guy you texted me about." I leaned forward and nudged her with my toe. "We already know that Quinn is hanging with some rich boy. What about you? Tell us all about your guy."

"I told you all there is to know about him already. I met someone," Cassie admitted, her cheeks going pink. "But he's got a girlfriend, so nothing is happening."

"Then you need a new guy," I said. I'd told her that earlier, but it was worth repeating, in my opinion. "There are tons of them down here. Just pick one."

Quinn picked up her orange juice. "Mackenzie's right. There's plenty of time left. Let's get you a new, unattached guy."

"See? We both agree," I said, pointing at Cassie. "You need to move on."

"No." Cassie crossed her arms. She might be a sweet girl, but when she said no? She meant it. Nothing would change her mind. "Tell me more about your secretive guy. Why are you all suspicious of him?"

I leaned back in my chair and stared off into the distance. I'd taken off my hat earlier, but now I was wishing I'd put it back on. All it would take was one person to realize who I was, and my relaxing vacation would be over. So would my time with Austin…

Well, crap. I slammed my hat back on. I couldn't risk that. "I'm keeping the hat on. I can't risk being seen right now." I sat up straight, then leaned closer. "He just acts like a guy who has a lot of secrets. You know?"

"You mean, kind of like you?" Quinn asked, eyeing me. She had a tinge of red across her cheekbones. Maybe because she'd been out and about with her dude the other day. "You're not telling him who you are, after all."

"He knows," I admitted, lowering my head. "He figured it out already."

"*What*?" Cassie squealed. "That's not good, Mac. What if he tells someone, or sells the story of you two?"

I shook my head. "He won't."

"How can you be so sure?" Quinn asked, her brow furrowed. "Mackenzie…I don't know about this. I thought he didn't know who you were."

Geez. Even Quinn looked worried. I got it, and I appreciated the concern. They were the best friends a girl like me could ask for, but I couldn't live my whole freaking life as if I couldn't risk being caught having fun. That wasn't fair to myself.

"He didn't at first, but he figured it out and let it slip." I shrugged. "If he was going to sell me out, don't you think the paps would be here right now snapping pics of me?"

Quinn peeked over her shoulder. Cassie stood up and searched the crowd, holding her hand over her eyes like a sun visor. She sat back down and looked at me. "Just because he didn't yet doesn't mean he won't, you know."

"I do know." I lifted my chin. "But I also know it's a risk I'm willing to take. I'm so freaking sick of being scared to live. I can't do it anymore. I won't. He might sell me out, but he might not. And I'm willing to take that chance, for the first time in a long time."

Quinn reached out and squeezed my hand. "And if he turns out to be a jerk, we'll kick his ass for you. Right, Cass?"

"Right." Cassie cleared her throat. "No matter what, we're here for you."

I smiled at them, my heart going all warm and gooey. These were my girls, and I loved them. They'd been there through it all. The lies. The tears. The heartache. And they'd be here with me through all this, too. Whether it ended good or bad. It's the one sure thing I could count on in life—them being by my side.

"I know. And I love you."

Quinn twisted her face up and made a sound, then spoke in a Southern accent. "Now, now. Let's not go getting all mushy and lovey-dovey. This is a vacation. It ain't nothing but fun and games."

I laughed. I might have said something similar to that on the plane in one of my supposed lectures. I think it was after Quinn thanked me for bringing them with me. "Please. I don't even talk like that anymore. I stopped when I became famous because my agent didn't want me to be typecast as a little Southern girl—and 'ain't' was the first word banned from my language."

"Yeah, but it's still fun to do," she said, grinning at me.

Cassie nodded. "It really is."

Our food came, and we all fell silent. Once the waitress left, I picked up my spoon and dug in. "You'll see, though. By the time this vacation is over, none of us will be the same. It's going to be legendary. Just remember: you both have to make sure you live it to its fullest, like I am. Promise me."

Cassie looked doubtful, but Quinn nodded in agreement.

"Oh, I am. I think you're right. James is…he's special. And I'm glad I met him," Quinn said, her cheeks going pink. "He's the complete opposite of me, and I like that about him. It'll help me relax a little bit during break."

Cassie gripped her fork tight. "And I'll be having fun in the sun, too. Don't worry about me."

"With your forbidden man?" I teased her. "Hey, if he's hitting on you, he can't be that happy, right?"

"He's not hitting on me," Cassie said. "We're just friends."

I pointed my spoon at her. "That's what they all say in the beginning."

Quinn laughed.

Cassie frowned. "It's true."

I had the feeling she wished it wasn't true. I wouldn't say as much, since I'd tortured her enough already. But I knew she had a crush on this Tyler guy, even if she didn't want to admit it. And Quinn had James, while I…

I had Austin.

And I couldn't freaking wait to see him again, even if he was hiding something from me. Nowadays, wasn't everyone hiding something from the world? If they said they weren't, they were lying. Everyone had secrets.

He could hide his all he wanted…as long as he hid my secrets, too.

A little while later, I leaned against the wall outside the hotel, my sun hat firmly in place and my big shades hiding my eyes. Austin had texted me earlier this morning, telling me to be ready for a day of fun in the sun—complete with the snorkeling he'd mentioned last night. I was more than ready for all that and more. Especially if the day ended with some hot sex.

I'd gotten a taste of him last night, and now? I wanted more.

The valet came over. "Can I get you your car, ma'am?"

"Oh, no thank you." I motioned toward the street. "I'm waiting for a friend to pick me up."

He bowed. "Have a great day."

"Thank you."

I turned to see a black Volkswagen pull up. Maybe early 2000's. I had a feeling, even before he stepped out, that this would be Austin. The car door opened, and out came my man. The valet started forward, but Austin waved him away with a smile. "I'm here for her."

The valet looked at me, frowned at Austin, and walked away.

"Hey," I said, grinning. My heart fluttered at the sight of him, like it always did.

"Hey, yourself."

He came up to me. His dark hair was spiked, and he wore a short-sleeved gray shirt with a dragon on the front and a pair of swim shorts. Black shades and shoes topped off the outfit. He looked effortlessly attractive and hot.

Ridiculously hot.

He came up to me, grabbed me by the hips, and hauled me up against that hard chest of his. I wrapped my hands around the back of his neck, smiling up at him. "I've been waiting for you."

"I know," he said, staring down into my eyes. "Am I allowed to kiss you in public, or is that not allowed?"

I tipped my head back and grinned. "I'll permit it this time."

He chuckled, then lowered his mouth to mine, knocking the breath out of me with his passionate kiss. His tongue darted in between my lips, brushing against mine, and his fingers flexed on my hips. He ended the kiss way too fast. "You ready?"

I buried my fingers in his hair. "Not really. I kind of want to go back upstairs instead. What do you think?"

"Uh-uh. Not happening." He dropped a quick kiss on my mouth, then stepped out of my arms, grabbing my wrists so he could disentangle himself. "You're following my rules today, and we're going snorkeling."

"You being bossy?"

"I am." He cocked a brow. "You got a problem with that?"

"Nope." I trailed a finger down his chest, stopping at the waistband of his shorts. "But after I obey your commands all day, do I get hot sex as a reward?"

He laughed. "I think I can handle that."

I brushed by him, swinging my hips as I went. I heard him suck in a deep breath, then he hurried past me to open the passenger door to his car. My heart sped up a little bit at the gentlemanly gesture.

God, what a cliché.

"Thank you."

"You're welcome," he said, shooting me another grin.

I settled into the seat, letting him shut the door for me. His car was ridiculously clean. It even had one of those little green air freshener things that hung from the shifter, which made me think he'd cleaned it for me. No man kept his car this spotless. There wasn't a single thing in it. Not an extra pair of shades or gum. Nothing.

He slid onto his seat, buckling with a *click*, then started it. "You ready?"

"Yeah." I tugged on my seatbelt. "How long do I have you today?"

"All day and night, if you want me." He shifted into gear and pulled out of the spot. "I'm off at the bar, and I don't have another gig until tomorrow night."

"I want to listen to you sing," I said, perking up. "I missed your show the other night. Will you be at the same bar?"

"Yep." He shifted again, his long fingers effortlessly moving over the knob. "It's the only place I sing, really. I don't have the time or desire to shop myself around."

"But why not?" I crossed my legs and looked in the rearview mirror for a tail. Old habits die hard. "You should totally try to get yourself out there."

67

He grinned. "Thanks, but no thanks."

"Why not travel a little bit? See the world, do a few gigs." I shrugged. "It would be fun, and you never know what will come of it."

His fingers tightened on the knob, going white at the knuckles, but the smile didn't slip from his face. "I can't spend my life travelling the world, hoping to be noticed by someone who will back me."

I tapped my fingers on the car door, not understanding him. How could he be so laid back about a talent he could be using? As if it didn't matter that he could hit it big? "Do you ever write your own songs?"

He stole a quick glance at me, obviously hesitant to answer my question. "Yeah. Sometimes."

"Ever sold any?"

He snorted. "Nope."

"I'd look at a few, if you'd let me." I shut my mouth. God, why had I offered that? What we had going between us had nothing to do with my work, and I liked that. "If you have any, I mean. Maybe I could even buy one."

He shook his head, his jaw flexing. "I didn't fuck you to sell you a song. They're mine, and you're not going to buy one because you feel the need to be nice to me."

"I'm not trying to be nice to you. I just thought—"

"You thought it would make me happy if you offered me a chance. I'm sure most people are usually happy when you do." He revved the engine. "But I'm not most people. All I want from you is what we're already doing. So stop trying to buy my songs to stroke my ego. I don't need it. I just need you."

My jaw dropped. He might be the first person to ever turn me down when I offered them a chance to advance themselves. For some reason, this made me inexplicably happy. He didn't even want to try and sell me a song. That had to mean something. Like, maybe he actually only wanted me for me.

He reached over and closed my jaw for me, chuckling. "I've surprised you, haven't I?"

"Well…yeah."

"I want you and only you. Is that a bad thing?"

The thought made me get lightheaded and grow warmer. Sure, he'd been refusing my help, but I liked that. "No. That's fine with me."

He pulled into a parking spot and shut off the car. He shoved my hat from my head and cupped my cheek. His gaze skimmed over me, sending jolts of desire through my blood. And the way he looked at me, his eyes narrowed and blazing heat, made me feel treasured. Cared for.

My eyelids drifted shut, waiting. Hoping. Wanting.

His mouth melded to mine, stealing all rational thought with nothing more than a kiss. It was ridiculous how much power this man held over me. I should be scared. I should push him away and save myself before it was too late. But instead, I pulled him closer.

Screw rational thought. It never did anyone any good, anyway. So…I kissed him.

I curled my fists over his shirt, holding him exactly where I wanted him, and opened my mouth to his. As he tasted me, deepening the kiss with a growl, I gave myself over to him. Not even bothering to try to hold back. What was the point? This was real, and I'd never felt more alive than I did now.

In his arms.

He pulled back, our breathing heavy and matched. He was killing me with all these short, hot kisses. Making me need more. "You're going to kill me before this week is over."

I let out a little laugh. At least I wasn't the only one wanting more. "I was just thinking the same thing about you."

"Well then." He kissed the tip of my nose. "I guess we're even, aren't we?"

"I guess so." I smiled up at him, feeling hesitant all of a sudden. Maybe it's because I actually, truly liked him. I cleared my throat and averted my eyes. "So…snorkeling, huh? Have you ever been snorkeling?"

"Uh, yeah." He shot me a funny look. Probably because

I'd changed the subject pretty abruptly. "You don't live in Key West and not spend half your life in the water."

"But you weren't born here."

"Nope." He opened his car door, but didn't slide out. Instead, he talked without me prompting him. "But I've been here almost all my life. Florida's been my home for longer than I can remember."

"I see." My heart sped up at the little tidbit of information he'd given me without me asking. Maybe I could do the same. Trust him a little bit. "Well, I grew up in south Texas—"

"Wait a second, I thought you were from the South."

"I am."

He snorted. "Texas isn't the South. It's in the west."

"Don't start with me, *mister*." I glowered at him. "Texas is the South, no matter what anyone else says."

He laughed. "Fine, I'll allow it. You were saying?"

I shot him one last dirty look at his slight on my home state. "I was *saying*, I haven't been back there in years. My mom still lives there, but I don't go there to visit her. Like, ever."

He looked at me for a moment, then slid out of the car without a word. For a second, I thought he was going to ignore what I'd said. But when he opened my car door for me, his brow was furrowed. "Wasn't there a messy divorce between your parents?"

I took a shaky breath. I hated reliving that part of my life. I'd been young and so trusting. I'd been too young to know better. Too young to fight back.

My dad had fought for me, thank God.

"Mac?" he asked, his voice low. The fact that he'd started using the name only my friends used wasn't lost on me. Did he know that? "You don't have to answer that if you don't want to. I didn't mean to pry. It's not part of our deal."

I cleared my throat and forced a bright smile. "You're fine. Sorry. I zoned out for a second. It's not exactly my favorite memory in the world, but yeah. That story, unfortunately, was true." I widened my smile even more, determined to look as if

I didn't care that the one person who was supposed to protect me had betrayed me. "It was a horrible custody battle that involved lots of money. I've tried to forget that portion of my life, though. Lots of bad memories."

And that's all I was going to say on that matter.

He nodded, throwing an arm over my shoulders. "Yeah, I get that. I have a few things I've purposely forgotten, too." He dragged a hand through his hair. "Some of the memories I probably shouldn't have let go of, and others were good moves. It's always hard to tell which is which, though, isn't it?"

I nodded. "It is," I agreed softly. I hesitated. "Are you still in touch with your parents?"

He rubbed his forehead. "My mom is gone, and my dad killed himself. So, no, I'm not in touch with them." He looked down at me, his jaw tight. "Like I said, it's not a pretty story. We both have fucked-up pasts, I'd say, so how about we leave them there?"

I bit down on my lip, trying to swallow my reply. I wanted to tell him how sorry I was. Show him some sympathy, but I had a feeling that's the last thing he would want. So I didn't. I nodded. "Okay. Sounds good. No more doom and gloom talk."

His fingers flexed on my shoulder, and he smiled at me. I could tell it was forced, though. "Sounds good. So…when's your next tour?"

"Over the summer." I wrapped my arm around his waist. I thought it would feel awkward, but it felt right. Like it was meant to be this way. My stomach did a little flip. "I just finished recording an album. I took a light course load this quarter so I'd have time to work."

He led me toward a small shack. It had a sign up that stated the cost of snorkeling, the rental fees, and a disclaimer that the company wasn't responsible for the safety of the snorkelers. I swallowed hard. It looked awfully…shady.

"You stopping in Florida?" he asked, his fingers running over my shoulder absentmindedly.

"I'm sure we will," I answered distractedly. An old guy

with no teeth and a tropic shirt stood in the shack, playing a game of cards with himself. "Margaritaville" played in the background. "Is this place safe?"

"Huh?" He let go of me and pulled out a wad of cash, thumbing through it and not looking up at me. "Yeah, of course. Frank is the best in Key West."

I eyed him skeptically, dropping my hand from his waist with no small amount of regret. I didn't want to stop touching him. It felt too good. "Uh, are you sure? He misspelled *peril.*"

He laughed. "Lighten up, sweetheart. It'll be fun, and we'll have the place to ourselves. If we went to a more commonly used place, we would have company. And eyes on us." He looked at me meaningfully. "And by *us*? I mean *you*. I wanted you to be able to relax and have fun without worrying about cameras and videos."

I released the breath I'd been holding. So he'd brought us here to allow for some privacy? That was both thoughtful and sweet. He kept surprising me. I liked that about him. "Thank you for being so understanding. I'll pay my half of the fee."

"No, you won't. Today's on me." He shrugged. "And it's not a big deal. I get wanting to stay out of the spotlight." He smiled at Frank, leaning down and resting his elbows on the counter, if you could call it that. It was technically a piece of dirty plywood. "Hey, Frank. We'd like to go snorkeling today."

The old man grinned a toothless smile. "Why, look what the cat drug in. I thought you swore off snorkeling the last time Rachel got stung by a jellyfish."

Rachel? Who the heck was she?

Austin stiffened. "Yeah, well, I changed my mind," he said evenly, not looking my way. "I'm here with a friend, and she's never been out in the water before. We'll need two kits and some uninterrupted privacy."

Frank looked at me, smacked his lips together, then set down the deck of cards. "That'll cost you, of course. Today's been busy."

He looked out in the cove for snorkeling. It was as empty

as the parking lot. "Of course it has," Austin said dryly, exchanging an amused glance with me. "How much do you want?"

Frank named a ridiculous price. I opened my mouth to bargain him down, but Austin beat me to it. "Make it half that amount, and I'll throw in a few free drinks at the bar for the next month."

"Deal." Frank cackled and flipped the OPEN sign over to CLOSED, then held out his hand. "Cash only, please."

"I've got it right here," Austin agreed. When I reached into my shorts pocket, he glowered at me. "Don't even think about it. I told you this one's on me."

I didn't think I could accept that. I always paid my way on dates. I could certainly afford it. "But—"

He handed his money over to the greedy old man. "My date suggestion. My money." He looked at me and crossed his arms, the stubbornness in his eyes clearly said he wouldn't budge. "Unless you'd rather go home…?"

I gritted my teeth. The way he took over without even letting me voice an opinion was so infuriating and yet so hot at the same time. He was so very alpha male. I hadn't thought I was into that type of thing, but judging from my primitive reaction to his arrogance? I was. I *really* was.

"I don't want to go home. But you already knew that, didn't you?"

He stepped closer, dropping his mouth to my ear level. I could feel his hot breath fanning over my skin, making my stomach clench tight. "Good. Because I plan on doing a lot more in that private cove than snorkeling, sweetheart."

I shivered and silently thanked God for small favors, because I was ready to explode if he didn't touch me soon. "We'll see about that."

"Indeed, we will." He traced the curve of my hip with his pinky. The soft touch did crazy things to my body. "Now follow me."

I was starting to think I'd follow him anywhere he asked.

CHAPTER

Austin

I kicked through the crystal clear water, watching Mackenzie as she swam up to a school of bright blue fish. The brilliant corals and anemone surrounded us on all sides, and she looked so damn beautiful with them as her backdrop. She held out her hand, letting the fish swim around it, and then wiggled her fingers animatedly.

Maybe I could have joined her in that moment. Extended my fingers, too. But I was too busy watching her to join in the fun. She mesmerized me more than any God-given creature ever had, and I wasn't sure what to do with that. I wasn't sure what to do with her at all. This was a fun fling with an expiration date.

We both knew it. Yet…

I was kind of sad I knew it.

For the first time in my fucking life, I felt a real connection to another person. She made me want to open up to her. To talk about things I'd never talked about, not even with Rachel. Hell, I even told her that my dad committed suicide. I never talked about that shit with anyone.

Again, not even with Rachel.

We acted as if it never happened, even though we both still had nightmares about that night. Shit like that tended to stay with you.

Mackenzie turned to me, her green eyes shining through the mask. She pointed up, and I nodded. We stuck our heads out of the water, I freed my mouth from the snorkel and took off my mask. She did the same. I swiped my hand over my mouth, my eyes on her the whole time.

I couldn't stop fucking watching her.

I felt like a teenager all over again. And the best part about this outing was that I'd get to spend all day with her. I couldn't be happier about that. Rachel was at a friend's house for the night, so I was free and clear to do what I wanted.

And I wanted Mackenzie.

"Oh my God, this is so much fun." She swam up to me and threw her arms around my neck, pressing her warm body against mine. She was so soft and smooth in all the places I was hard and rough. "Thank you for suggesting this."

"You're welcome, Mac." I pressed my hand against her lower back, fingers splayed, and slid my hand down to her legs. I hauled her up against me, urging her legs around my waist. "But I can think of an even better way for you to thank me."

Her eyes went wide, but then she hooked her ankles behind my back. "Oh?" she asked breathlessly, her lips pursed. "And what would that be?"

"A kiss wouldn't be the worst thing in the world, that's for sure."

She played with a piece of hair on the back of my head, tugging enough to set my blood to boiling. "I might be able to arrange that…if you ask really nicely."

"I don't ask nicely," I said, slipping my hand between her

JEN McLAUGHLIN

legs. "But I do know how to get results."

She laughed. "I—"

I growled playfully and crashed my lips to hers, cutting her off. She tasted like salt water and Mackenzie—sweet and salty at the same time. Like perfection. Her teeth pressed into my lips, and her tongue dipped inside my mouth. As she swirled it around mine, making a small sound in the back of her throat, I cupped her ass, holding her against my cock.

Holding her just because it felt good.

I deepened the kiss, spinning so I kind of rested against the sand bed behind me, supporting our weight easily. Her nails skimmed over my shoulders and down my pecs, digging in just enough to hurt so fucking good. In the back of my mind, I knew we should stop. Even though this was a private cove, it was far from secure.

I ended the kiss. "Anyone could be watching, and with a public face like yours, you can never—"

She slid her hand between us and cupped my cock...and I forgot all about being cautious. All that mattered was us. This. She trailed her fingers over the length of me, then closed her hand over the tip of my cock. As she squeezed, tugging with the perfect amount of pressure, I sucked my lower lip into my mouth, biting down gently.

She might have been a virgin when we met, but damn, she was good.

When she let out a breathy moan and repeated the motion, I slipped my hands between her thighs. I pressed the pad of my three fingers into her, rolling them in slow circles over her. "*Austin*," she breathed, pressing closer to my fingers. "More."

I loved when she whispered my name like that, all breathless and sexy. I could play that on repeat for the rest of my life and die with a smile on my face. I captured her mouth with mine, increasing the pressure on her clit with my fingers. I wished I could go down on her right here.

Bury myself inside of her.

But we didn't have protection, and we definitely didn't have

76

privacy. So I had to content myself with this. With some grade school, third base shit. With my free hand, I rolled her nipple between my fingers, breaking off the kiss to bite down on her shoulder at the same time. "You drive me fucking insane," I said, nipping the spot directly over her pulse. "You're so damn sexy, sweetheart."

She threw back her head. The graceful arch of her neck captivated me. Hell, *she* captivated me. She was getting her grips on me, deep and painful, and there wasn't a fucking thing I could do to stop it. I couldn't look away. Couldn't hold her off. Hell, I didn't even want to try.

I was a train wreck waiting to happen.

Her fingers moved over me more insistently, and I did the same to her. Our heavy breathing matched perfectly, as if we were in tune with one another without even trying. And the crazy thing was, I did feel that way with her.

As if we had more than sex and passion between us...

Which was stupid.

I closed off those thoughts and filed them away for a later date. Maybe when I was older and wiser, I'd be ready for them. But not now.

"Don't stop," she begged, her legs tightening around me. "God, don't stop."

I could feel her whole body growing tighter and straining against me. Knowing she was that close to coming sent me teetering on the edge. I'd have never thought I could come from some heavy petting and kisses, but with Mackenzie...

Apparently all I needed was a hand job and a smile.

I grunted and moved faster, my hips pumping into her hand at the same time. I knew the second she found her pleasure. Knew when time froze for her, because her hand clenched down on my cock, and she let out a little sound deep in the back of her throat.

I loved that fucking sound.

Then I closed my eyes and dropped my head into the crook of her neck. I could finish. I really could, with just her hand

and a kiss. But when I did come, I wanted to be buried inside her, damn it. I wanted to be inside of her, making her scream my name and scratch my back. So I headed for the shore with her still in my arms, juggling my equipment and her with ease.

"Where are we going?" she asked, resting her head on my shoulder.

Her mask and snorkel hit my back. She'd managed to hang on to them, even with me making her fall apart. "To my car so I can fuck you properly." As we passed Frank, I tossed the snorkeling equipment his way. Then I set her down on her feet. "Lose the flippers."

She held on to the shack, squirming out of them. I did the same, then caught her hand with mine. We padded barefoot to the car, since we'd left our shoes and extra clothing inside, and I opened the back door. I'd parked in a shady, secluded section of the parking lot and I couldn't be happier about that, because I needed her now.

I pushed her onto her back, reaching into the console and pulling out a condom. I'd thrown them in there earlier just in case. As I yanked my trunks down, I stopped, my hand on my cock. She was watching me with wide eyes.

She flicked her tongue over her lips, her thighs falling open. "Hurry up," she said, moving impatiently.

Still…I hesitated. Damn it. She deserved better than a quick fuck in the car.

She was Mackenzie Forbes—America's Sweetheart—not some girl I'd picked up at the bar who didn't give a damn how or where she got it, or even who she got it from. She'd been a virgin yesterday, and now I was about to take her in the back of my fucking Volkswagen? *Pathetic, Austin.*

It was no wonder guys like me never got girls like her.

I started pulling up my shorts. "You know what? We can wait. Let's go back to the hotel and—"

"No." She yanked me back down on top of her. My cock pressed against her pussy, and she arched her hips up. Not exactly helping my resolve to give her something better than a quickie in a parking lot, for fuck's sakes. "I don't want to wait."

She closed her fingers over me, gazing up at me with wonder. Well, *hell*, if she kept looking at me as if she needed me to fuck her, I wouldn't be responsible for my actions. And for the first time in a long time, I wanted to be responsible. I wanted to be a gentleman, damn it. "I'm trying to be a good guy here."

"I don't want you to be good. I want you to be bad." She flicked her tongue over my lips, and I squeezed my eyes shut. "Really, *really* bad."

"Someone might come along," I said through my clenched teeth. "I'm trying to protect you."

"Then you better hurry up so no one finds us." I swallowed hard, my eyes skimming over her perfection. The freckles on her nose. The bright green eyes. Her full rosy pink lips. She looked even hotter in the natural light of day, if that was possible. "Between us? I think you're perfectly capable of making me scream your name in less than five minutes."

I ripped open the condom wrapper, using my teeth. "You're sure?"

"God, yes." She spread her legs and shoved her bottoms to the side, giving me a hell of a view of her wet pussy. Fuck. There went the last of my gentlemanly thoughts, right out the fucking window. "Take me now."

I growled, rolled the condom over my cock, then fell on top of her. I was wedged up against this side of heaven, my forehead to hers, and I couldn't imagine any place I'd rather be. And that fucking terrified me.

I thrust inside of her, my whole body seeming to let out a sigh. I kissed her and started moving faster. Harder. She wrapped herself around me, and the stinging of her nails raking across my back sent me over the edge.

So did the little whimpers she kept letting out, soft and sweet. Better than any song I'd ever fucking heard. I kissed her again, swallowing her cries of pleasure so no one heard her, and completely lost myself in her. Her pussy clenched tighter around my cock, squeezing, but it wasn't enough.

I reached between us and pressed two fingers against her clit. I was fucking bent on making her explode again before I came. By the time I was finished with her, I was determined to be her best memory of this town—of this trip.

God knows she would be mine.

She cried out, arching her back, and tensed all around me, releasing my name on a sigh. "Austin."

Music to my ears, man.

I thrust into her one more time, my balls going tight and hard, and then I came so strongly my vision blurred. "God," I muttered, dropping my head down beside hers and drawing in a shaky breath. She was going to kill me. It was official.

And if she didn't kill me, she was going to get me arrested. Hell, I hadn't gotten naked in a fucking car with a woman in years. Not since I'd started taking care of Rachel.

I had to remember I had responsibilities.

"Wow," she breathed, playing with my hair. "I was teasing about the 'orgasm in less than five minutes' part, but you totally did it."

I snorted and lifted up on my elbows. I might want to lay here and enjoy the afterglow, but we had to get dressed. "Maybe I should start a business. 'Orgasms delivered in less than five minutes, guaranteed or your money back.'"

"Umm…" She laughed, musical and perfect, of course. Because it was *her*. "I think I'd rather keep you to myself forever and ever. You just might be my best-kept secret, and I'm not about to blab about you to everyone."

I knew she was fucking around, but hearing her talk about any kind of future set me on edge. There wasn't a future with us. There couldn't be.

She wouldn't want me once she knew the real me, and all my secrets that came with me. And she definitely wouldn't want a teenager in her life—and Rachel was part of me now. She wouldn't want a fuck-up with a buried juvenile criminal record either.

And I needed to remember that before it was too late.

"Yeah." I pushed off her, not quite meeting her eyes. "I kind of figured that."

"Hey," she said, sitting up and fixing her bikini bottoms. I did the same with my trunks, the cold wetness making me shiver. "You okay?"

I looked at her. "Yeah. Of course."

"O…kay." She tucked her hair behind her ear, peeking up at me. "You just got all stiff and withdrawn or something."

I shrugged. "Nah. But we should probably get out of here before we get caught."

"Yeah, probably." She leaned in and rested her palm against my cheek, her thumb sliding down to my dimple. "Today was really special. Thank you."

I swallowed hard. The feelings rolling through me had nothing to do with sex and everything to do with the forbidden. I couldn't want her. Couldn't want more.

But I also couldn't pull away.

She leaned closer, hesitating briefly with her lips hovering close to mine. Giving me a chance to reject her, I supposed. Maybe I should have, but I didn't. Her eyes lit up, and then she kissed me tenderly. This kiss felt different. It wasn't about arousal or sex.

And I loved every second of it.

CHAPTER *Nine*

Austin

*T*hanks to the fact that Rachel was spending the night at a friend's house, Mackenzie and I had spent the last few hours talking and snuggling in the privacy of her hotel room. And now we were at a restaurant I'd never taken another girl to besides Rachel. I couldn't help but notice I kept bringing Mac to my favorites. As if I was trying to show her a part of me I didn't normally show girls.

I tried to ignore this fact, too.

"You come here a lot?" she asked, looking over her shoulder. "I love the décor. Very modern yet elegant."

I looked around, trying to see what she saw. Crystal chandeliers hung over all the tables, and candles flickered on each one. Soft music played in the background, and everyone spoke quietly amongst themselves. Everyone was chill and relaxed. No one rushed or hurried through their meals. That's why I loved it here. In a life of hectic-ness and bar music, the understated peacefulness of this restaurant called to me.

"Yeah. It's nice." I lifted a shoulder. "And tourists don't come here, so it's not overcrowded."

She nodded. "It's perfect for a girl like me."

"Right." I met her eyes. "No cameras."

"Exactly."

We fell silent, and she picked up her glass and gulped some wine down. I watched her, loving the way the candlelight flickered across her face. "Are you having fun down here in Florida? Doing all the things you wanted to do? Seeing it all?" I picked up my beer. "If there's something else you'd like to do besides see me naked, maybe I could take you sightseeing."

She smiled at me, soft and sweet. "You'd do touristy stuff with me?"

It sounded like pure hell, but I'd be with her—which was as close to heaven as I'd ever get. "Sure. Why not?"

"Nothing. It's just…" She entwined her ankle with mine underneath the table. "It's just sweet is all."

I snorted. There she went using inappropriate words to describe me again. I almost pulled my ankle away from hers to protest her descriptors, but it felt too damn good. "I'm not fucking sweet."

"What's the matter?" Her smile widened. "Does that not fit the bad boy image you try so hard to put out there?"

She was teasing me. Actually fucking teasing me. Two can play at that game.

"Oh, you can call me 'sweet' if it makes you happy. As a matter of fact…" I leaned in and motioned for her to do the same. She moved closer, and her lower lip was caught between her teeth, as if she was nervous or turned on—or both. "I'll show you how sweet I can be when I bend you over the trunk of my car and fuck you until you scream. How's that sound?"

Her eyes flared. "It sounds perfect." She released her lower lip, and I couldn't stop staring at the red mark she left behind. "But being good at dirty talk doesn't make you any less sweet.

83

It just makes you the total package."

I blinked at her. She was fucking insane. If she thought I was the total package, she seriously needed to re-evaluate her standards. "Yeah. Not so much."

"You don't see you for what you really are."

"I was about to say the same thing to you. You think I'm something I'm not."

Something I'd like to be for her.

"No, I don't." She played with her bread, then looked up at me with those gorgeous green eyes of hers. "Austin?"

"Yeah?"

"Would you like to maybe keep in touch? You know, after."

Hell yeah, I did. But was it for the best? I didn't do this. And she didn't know what she was agreeing to. She knew nothing about me. But still...

Maybe it was time she found out.

"Mackenzie." I reached across the table and held her hand, letting myself stop the worrying for a second. "I—"

I cut myself off when my phone rang. It was lying on the table between us, face up. We both glanced at it, me to see who it was. Her probably out of habit more than anything else. The name on the front couldn't have been any clearer.

It was Rachel.

"I'm sorry, but I've gotta get this." I grabbed my phone and didn't meet her eyes. I got out of my seat, headed for the door, and answered. "What's up, Rach?"

"Okay, don't be too mad, but we left Kaitlyn's house for a party, and it's bad, Austin. Drinking. Drugs. Sex." She took a shuddering breath. "I didn't know it was going to be like this, and you said to call if I ever needed you to come get me from a bad situation—no questions asked."

I closed my eyes, making myself bite back the reprimands I wanted to give her. She was supposed to be having a laid-back sleepover, not going to some crazy party. Hell, I wanted to fucking scream at her. Behind me, I could barely make out the sound of Mac laughing lightly at something the waiter said.

84

"You went to that party I refused to let you go to, didn't you?"

She sniffed. "Yeah. And I know I'm grounded. But can you please come get me and *then* ground me?"

"Yeah," I bit out. I was proud of her for calling me for help. I really was. But I was also fucking pissed at her for lying to me. "Where are you?"

She named the address. It was about five minutes past Mackenzie's hotel. After promising to be there in ten minutes, I hung up and turned around. Mackenzie still sat at the table, fiddling with her wineglass. When I came back to her side, she looked up at me and stood. She wrapped her arms around herself, watching me without saying a word. I shoved my phone into my pocket and dragged a hand through my hair. "Mac…"

"Let me guess? You have to go?" she asked, her tone level.

"Yeah." I hesitated. "It's a long story, and I'll give it to you, but right now? I don't have time. I have to hurry up."

"I figured. I already paid the bill while you were on the phone."

I stiffened. "I can pay the damn bill."

"I'm sure you can, but I did it already." She headed for the door, sliding into the dark night without a backward glance.

I followed her, my hands fisted. I was going to fucking ground Rachel for life after this. No questions asked. I unlocked the car, and she took her seat without a word. I got into the car, too, starting it with an angry jerk of my hand.

"Are you going to tell me what's going on?" she asked, her voice perfectly steady. "And who's Rachel?"

I pulled out of the spot, gripping the wheel tight. "It's a complicated answer. One I really don't feel like giving you when I'm so angry I could fucking scream. You'll have questions. There's not enough time to cover them."

She gripped her thighs. "I see. Is she your girlfriend?"

"*No.*" She was picking a fight when I didn't have the time to take my part in it. "Do you honestly think I'd be fucking you if I had a girl waiting for me back home?"

"I didn't think so, no," she said softly. "So who is she?"

My phone dinged again, so I glanced at it. Rachel had texted me. *I'm outside waiting. Hurry, please. I love you.* I glanced at Mac, and she was watching me. "Look, I—"

"You don't have to say another word. You have secrets, and I totally get that." She lifted her hand, but dropped it back in her lap. "But maybe we should quit while we're ahead. We had fun. You were nice, and no one got hurt. Maybe this should be the end. I have a feeling if it's not, it might not go so good in the end. I already feel more than I should, and it's only going to get more intense. This was supposed to be easy and fun, but it doesn't feel that way anymore."

"No, it doesn't." I stopped at the red light, anger coursing through my veins. "I don't think it ever did, though. Nothing in life comes easy."

She nodded, gazing out the window. The rest of the ride passed in silence. I kept wanting to break it, to give her an explanation of some sort, but what was the point? There wasn't enough time, and she'd already come to her senses and called things off with me. Why bore her with the details of my shitty past now?

As I pulled up to the hotel, she put her hand on the knob, looking at me one last time. She seemed to be giving me a chance to say something. Anything.

"I had fun today," I said lamely.

She pressed her lips together. "Me too. Goodbye, Austin."

And she got out, shutting the door behind her. I knew she was saying goodbye for forever, and I also knew it was for the best. There was nothing I could do about it.

I had to go save my sister…again.

CHAPTER

Mackenzie

I looked up at the ceiling, studying the crack that ran all the way across it. It had been a long night and morning, ever since Austin and I had parted ways, and I was going a little bit crazy. Luckily, Cassie was here now to distract me from my thoughts. "And then he told me he had to go."

"But why?" Cassie asked, propping her chin in her hand and studying me.

"This Rachel person, whoever that is." I shrugged. "He says it's not his girlfriend, but I'm just not sure what to think anymore."

"Yeah. That sounds confusing." Cassie fidgeted with her light blonde hair. "Maybe it's an ex he still has feelings for?"

"Yeah, maybe." I sighed. "Either way, it's over. I told him we should call it quits while we were ahead, and he didn't argue with me."

Cassie reached out to squeeze my hands. "I'm sorry, Mac. I know you liked him a lot."

"I did, but maybe that's why it's a good thing we ended it now. If I hung around him much more, I might have been hooked on him even more, you know?"

After all, I was already missing him too much as it was. That wasn't what I wanted. I wanted easy. Carefree. Spring fling. Not this undying need to see him again.

"Yeah, you were quite clear you didn't want any long-term crap going on." Cassie grinned, but it looked a little bit forced. "You also forbade us from attaching ourselves to anyone."

"Yeah." I hesitated. "Speaking of which, how's Tyler? You still hanging around him?"

Her cheeks turned red. "Yeah."

"And does he still have a girlfriend?"

"Well, I'm not sure." She sat up and gripped her knees. "I'm going to find out 'everything' later tonight. What 'everything' is…I have no idea."

"You seem nervous. You think it's bad?"

She looked at me, then glanced away. "It's been kind of crazy, honestly. There was some drugging of girls going on, and somehow I got in the middle of it, and now—"

I held up a hand. "Wait just a second. Drugging? And you were involved?"

"Yeah. I kind of sort of got targeted last night."

I gasped and covered my mouth, then hauled her close for a hug. "Oh my God, Cassie. Why didn't you tell us?" I scrambled for my phone. "I should call Quinn. She needs to hear this. Did you tell her yet?"

"No." She grabbed my phone out of my hand. "She's out having fun, and I'm fine. I didn't tell you because I didn't want to ruin your vacation, and Tyler took care of me. It was scary, but I'm fine. I swear. Don't bug her."

"All right. I won't call her." I sat up straighter and threw my arm over her shoulder, hugging her close. "But I need more details, please. Every. Single. One."

As I listened to my best friend fill me in on everything I'd missed, I realized this is what I should have been doing all along. We'd all come down here, determined to let loose and have fun, and we'd missed so much of each other's lives in the process.

It was time to focus on being myself again...and to focus on my girls.

A few hours later, my phone rang. I picked it up off the bed and peeked at the caller. It wasn't who I was hoping for, of course. Austin wasn't calling, and I had to face the facts. He'd been fine with me ending things, and I had to face *that*, too.

Sighing, I hit *decline*. It was my agent...again. I wasn't in the mood to talk shop.

I looked out the window, watching the rain pour down. Lightning struck, and I flinched. It was nasty out there tonight. Good thing I was staying in. Cassie was out on a date with Tyler. Quinn was with James. And I was...

Here. Alone. Again.

I tapped my fingers on my MacBook Air, debating what to do. Maybe I would Google Austin's name and see what came up. It would occupy my time, if nothing else. I slammed the lid down, angry with myself for even *thinking* about Googling him.

He deserved to keep his secrets. Just because I could barely keep my bra size private didn't mean he didn't have his civil rights. And I couldn't begrudge him that. If he'd wanted to tell me about this Rachel girl, then he would have. If he wanted to be done with me, after I'd told him we were done, then he could be done.

And I'd have to accept that.

But there was something about him that called for me to know more. Heck, to know everything. I wanted to know his hopes, dreams, and fears. I wanted to know his past and maybe even be in his future. But that wasn't possible…was it?

My phone vibrated and I reached for it with a racing heart. Maybe it would be a text from Austin, even though we'd "broken up." It wasn't. It was my head of security, and they'd dug up Austin's past, judging from the title of the email: Intel on Austin Murphy.

Well, crap. Should I open it?

If I really wanted to respect his privacy, I couldn't. I shut off the screen, tossing my phone out of arm's reach. I couldn't stop staring at it. All it would take was a quick scan through the email and I'd have all the answers I needed about him. I'd know why he was so closed off and cautious. I'd know all his secrets.

But at what cost?

A knock sounded on the door, and I rolled off the bed. It was probably Cassie again. Maybe she'd come to tell me more about Tyler and his big secret. I could certainly use the distraction. I started talking even before I opened the door. "Cass, did you find out—"

I broke off the second I had the door open, my eyes going wide. It wasn't Cassie. It was Austin, and he was soaking wet. He almost looked like a criminal, all haggard and wet and disheveled. His black ink stood out against the backdrop of his pale, wet, goosebump-covered skin.

If I'd passed him on the road looking this way, I'd have steered clear. Now…I couldn't look away. "You came back."

"I shouldn't have. You told me you were done with me, and I tried to respect that. But they had me on the approved visitors list. I guess you put me there at one point?"

I nodded. I'd added him to the list after breakfast yesterday, figuring he'd come up to see me at some point this week. "I did."

"Well, I'm glad." He dragged his hands down his face. "Because I can't fucking stay away from you unless you kick me out. Tell me to leave right now—or let me in. Your choice."

As if there was a question of which one I'd choose. I

opened the door, stepping back to let him in. "Did you walk here in the rain?"

"Yeah." He walked in and shut the door behind him. "I needed to clear my head."

He yanked off his drenched shirt, and I swallowed hard. His muscles flexed and stretched to perfection, making me itch to touch him. But I didn't.

"Oh." I bit down on my lip. "Why are you here?"

He wiped his shirt over his wet face, watching me the whole time. He looked so dangerously sexy that the freaking smoke alarms should be ringing.

How was I supposed to resist him?

"I'm here for you. To talk, since you obviously want to, or need to. Go ahead. Ask me anything." He dropped the shirt. "And I'll answer."

Talk? Seriously? All I could think about was jumping him, and he finally wanted to talk? I swallowed the half-hysterical laugh that tried to bubble out. "Okay. So talk. Tell me what happened today."

"I don't tell people about myself, and I don't bond. I don't ever want more than a quick fuck and a goodbye." He leaned against the wall. "I didn't want a relationship. And neither did you, and we said that from the beginning. But we keep talking about shit that has nothing to do with fucking, which makes me think you want more."

I nodded. He was right, but I didn't know what to say to that.

He continued on without an answer from me. I guess he didn't need one. "You're cautious about who you hang out with. I get it." He crossed his arms. "But I kind of liked you not knowing much about me, to be honest. The locals know all about me. They know what I did, and who I am. They know it all."

I tensed. Is this the part where he told me he was a serial killer or something? No. That couldn't be true. Not my Austin. He was rough around the edges, but he wasn't a criminal.

"What did you do?"

"It's more what I didn't do."

"Okay." I bit down on my inner cheeks, trying to remain calm. "What didn't you do?"

"I didn't protect her." He let out a frustrated sound. "Rachel isn't my girlfriend." He tossed his shirt across the room. It landed on the couch. "She's my sister, and I'm basically her dad now."

I digested that. After hearing bits and pieces of his life, I hadn't even considered the fact that he'd had siblings. Stupid, really. Why wouldn't he? "Wow."

"Yeah. But it's true. She's more like my child at this point. I'm a dad to a teenager. Let that sink in." He rubbed the back of his neck and looked at me, his face impassively cool. "She's sixteen, but I've been her guardian since she was fourteen. Ever since my father blew his brains out in front of her." Austin laughed uneasily, not meeting my eyes. "Yeah, you heard that right. But he took a few shots at her first. Tried to take her down with him. Good thing he was too high to see clearly."

"Oh my God…" I swallowed the bile rising to my throat. I knew his father had killed himself, but in front of his own child? And he'd tried to kill her, too? That was horrible. No wonder he didn't want to talk about it. "I'm so sorry."

He cocked his head. "Why do people apologize for something they didn't do? I never got that. You weren't the one who wasn't there to save her from him. That was all me. *I* was the one who failed her. *I* was the one who wasn't there to save her from his fucking selfishness. Not you."

"You couldn't have known—"

He held up a hand. "Oh, trust me. I knew how much of an asshole he was. It's why I left in the first place. I'd been beaten, broken, and abused more times than I could count before I turned fourteen. That's when I started fighting back. That's when I ran away, too. I should have stolen her and taken her with me. That was my biggest mistake, and I'll never make up for the fact that I left her behind."

I blinked back tears, my throat throbbing. "Was she with him when you left?"

"No, she was living with my mom at that point. But then she left…and I didn't go back to save Rachel from my dad." He shook his head, his face scrunched up as he remembered. "I failed her."

I wanted to take it all away. Make it all better, but I also knew I couldn't. I couldn't save him from his demons, no matter how much I wanted to. "Austin."

"I tried to pretend she was fine back in Florida when I was in California trying to get signed at a record label," he said, meeting my eyes. "I lived in denial for a long time. I tried to live in my own fucking bubble, promising myself that when I made it big, she would come out with me. I'd treat her like a princess." He placed a hand over his heart. "That guilt is on *me*. That is who I am—the jerk who ran away from his own sister."

"No." I shook my head and went up to him, cupping his face. Tears filled my eyes, but I tried to blink them back. "This wasn't your fault. You were too young to comprehend the consequences of your actions. When you were an adult, you came back. You take care of her now, and that's all that matters."

"Pretty words from a pretty girl." His lips twisted. "But it was my fault. I was the one who was in L.A. recording a fucking demo, with big dreams and aspirations. If I'd have stayed with her—" He broke off, then gripped my hands so tight it almost hurt. "I wasn't there, Mackenzie. I failed her. And I'm going to fail you, too. Just wait and see."

I rose on tiptoe and pressed a kiss to his jaw. "No, you're not. There won't be enough time to fail me," I joked, trying to lighten the mood. I kissed his dimple. If only kisses made it all better, like when I'd been a child. "I leave soon, remember?"

"Don't remind me," he groaned. "I'm no good for you, but fuck if I don't want to be." He turned his face into mine. "I'm a selfish bastard, and I don't want to let you go yet."

He'd had a horrible life. A hard life.

I wanted to make his future brighter in any way I could, for what little time we had together, but I couldn't keep making him talk about stuff. I lifted up on tiptoe, and he framed my face with his hands. And then he kissed me.

And what a kiss it was.

Stars burst in front of my eyes at the force of his mouth on mine. I wrapped my hands behind his neck, yanking him even closer, and he swung me into his arms effortlessly. We'd kissed before, plenty of times. But this time it felt different.

This was warm and sweet and full of promise.

He walked to my bed, laying me down on it gently. He stood back, his gaze skimming over my body. I wished I was wearing something more seductive than a countrified plaid shirt and a pair of shorts, but that's who I was. A country girl at heart.

And he was the bad boy who'd come to rescue me. Who needed a prince when men like Austin existed? Prince Charming was *so* overrated.

Give me a man like Austin any day.

"We barely know each other." He crawled up my body. "But I've told you more about myself in one fucking day than I have anyone else ever. Just wanted to mention that. You're special to me. You have been since the moment you walked into my bar."

My throat threatened to close up on me. Knowing that he felt the same way I did was insane. I didn't believe in love at first sight. Heck, I barely believed love was real. But for the second time in as many days, the same thought crossed my mind. With him I could totally see it happening. I could believe in it.

I could write a song about it.

He closed his mouth over my nipple, and even through the fabric of my shirt and bra, I felt his heat. I squirmed and buried my hands in his hair. Parts of me wanted to simply take what he had given me, and lose myself in his touch.

But he'd opened up to me. Shouldn't I do the same for him?

I wanted to give him more of myself than I'd ever given anyone else—just like he had with me. Even the playing ground, so to speak. "I...I want to tell you something, too. Something I haven't told anyone else. Not even my best friends, who know *every*thing about me."

He lifted his head, his smoky eyes meeting mine. "What's that?"

"My mom didn't just divorce my dad and try to keep me in her custody. She was a drug addict. Cocaine. She snorted half my bank account up her nose, and then wanted more. We managed to keep it a secret from the media, but I'm not sure how." I took a deep breath, not dropping his gaze. "I haven't heard from her in years. I hate her for what she did to me. I hate her for what she did to herself, too. But mostly...I just hate her."

Holy crap. I hadn't ever admitted that last part to anyone. Not even myself.

CHAPTER
Eleven

Austin

C held my breath, unable to believe the sweet country princess of America had uttered those words to me. That she could hate, when all I'd seen out of her was happiness and sunshine, for the most part. Or maybe it just seemed that way, since she made me feel so fucking alive. But either way, I couldn't believe it.

"I had no idea," I finally managed to say. "My dad was all about heroin, not cocaine. He had a thing for getting so wasted he couldn't even talk, let alone stand up straight. And then the hallucinations. He thought my sister was a cop. That's why he tried to shoot her."

"I think my mom had those, too." She reached out and smoothed my hair off my forehead. I closed my eyes, enjoying her tender touch. If she let me, I could lose myself in Mackenzie and never come back out. "She never tried to shoot us, but she was acting all kinds of crazy during the court hearings. Accusing us of all kinds of insane stuff."

I let out a breath. "Sounds like we had similar lives."

And the weird thing was...we did.

She might be rich and famous now, but she had gone through the same fucked-up childhood I had. Hers had just ended happy while mine hadn't. That was the only difference between us. "A little bit, yeah," she said.

"We're either really good for each other," I kissed her gently, making sure not to linger for too long, "or we're going to fuck each other up even more than we already are."

She trailed her hands down my back. It felt so fucking good it was stupid. "We only have a couple of days to do our damage, one way or the other."

That was the third time she'd said as much in the space of a few minutes. Was she reminding me of that, or herself? I wasn't going to beg her to stay, if that's what she was worried about. When it came time to say goodbye, I'd fucking say goodbye and walk away. End of story. I could only imagine she would do the same.

"So your sister...does she listen to my music?"

I chuckled. "Yeah. She idolizes you. I took her to one of your concerts last year."

"Wow. If I had seen you then..." She skimmed her fingers up my back, keeping close to my spine. "This would've happened a year earlier, I bet."

"Or not." I clenched my hands on her ass, rolling my hips against her. I had no experience with virgins and how they might feel after two rounds of sex. "I would've had my sister with me, after all."

"It wouldn't have mattered. I'd have found a way to woo you into my bed."

"Speaking of which..." I nibbled on her neck, my pulse racing. Fuck, I wanted her naked *now*. And more than sex, I wanted her. That might not make much sense, but to me it did. "Are you too sore for me to fuck you again?"

"Nope." She wrapped her legs around my waist. "Even if I was, I wouldn't care. We don't have enough time to worry about sore body parts."

"There's never enough time," I agreed, capturing her lips. "Not when it comes to this."

And it was true.

There would never be a time where I'd have enough of her. I knew it to the bottom of my blackened soul. I kissed her, letting my hands roam over her body. Sometimes, I swore I already knew all the hills and valleys of her curves.

I knew she liked it when I hooked my arm under her knee and thrust into her deep and hard. I knew she went crazy when I bit her neck. And I knew that when she came, she always let out the same adorable little moan. And I knew no matter how many times I said it, what we had going on between us was more than just sex.

I just didn't want to admit it.

She called to me in a way I'd never felt before. As if she'd been meant for me and only me. The real kicker was I couldn't have her. Even if we decided to make a go of it, which she hadn't given any indication whatsoever of wanting to do, we would never work out.

She would go back to Chicago and jet across the country. And I'd be here. She'd be out partying and smiling at the cameras. And, once again, I'd be *here*.

The end of every scenario of her fabulous life ended with me staying here with Rachel. And that was fine. It's what I'd signed on for when I took over Rachel's guardianship. But it didn't make saying goodbye any easier.

The whole time I made love to Mac, all I could think about was this one fucking detail: Even if we hadn't separated, it was already over.

We'd never work.

CHAPTER

Austin

*I*t had been a night from heaven so far. We'd been in bed ever since this afternoon, and if I had my way? We'd never fucking leave it again. As soon as we left this room, real life would come crashing back to us. I didn't want that.

Didn't want to deal with the shit I knew we'd have to deal with.

As soon as I left, I would have to be Austin, big brother to Rachel. Always responsible. Always there. I wouldn't be Austin, hot bartender who Mackenzie Forbes picked. I wouldn't be this version of myself. I'd be ordinary.

It might be after midnight, but I was refusing to get up and leave. Refusing to be me. I rolled on top of her and kissed her, trying to shut my mind off. Trying to ignore that inner voice that mocked me for being me. And afterward, as I lay on top of her, my breath coming out heavy from the mind-blowing orgasm I'd just had, I closed my eyes against the overhead light above her bed.

She hugged me close. Fucking hugged me. Why did that affect me more than the earth-shattering sex? It didn't make any sense. "Can you stay the whole night?" she asked. "Or do you have to go home to Rachel?"

"I have my neighbor at my house watching her, so I'm good. She's kind of like a mother to us. The closest thing we have, anyway." I sighed and lifted up on my elbows, fairly certain my fucked-up feelings were sufficiently hidden from her. "Rachel's old enough to be alone, obviously, but I wanted someone to keep an eye on her after the whole party thing."

She nodded and reached out, smoothing my hair. "What happened earlier?"

"She told me she was going to her friend's house, but instead she went to a party I'd told her she couldn't go to. Turned out, I was right about it being bad news." I clenched my jaw, getting angry all over again. "There was drugs, sex, and booze, but at least she was smart enough to call me and get help."

"She could have lied and gotten a cab," Mackenzie said, smiling. "It shows how much she loves you that she called you and admitted her mistake."

"Yeah, I guess." I shrugged and rolled off her. I landed on my back, and rested my hands over my stomach. I always hurried out of the room after sex. Was always in a rush to leave the scene, so to speak. To get home. For once, I didn't want to fucking move, and I'd been here almost all night. "I think she wanted to get in trouble, maybe. Wanted to own up to the lie."

"Is she grounded for life?"

"Nah. Just for a month." I turned by head toward her. She was on her back, too, her dark hair splayed all across the pillow. Her green eyes were soft and warm. Her lips swollen from my kisses. I wanted to take a picture so I could remember this moment forever, but that wouldn't be permitted. No pictures. No news stories. "She came to me. Like you said, it was a mature decision. I didn't want to punish her too strictly after that."

"Maybe that was her goal all along," Mackenzie said, laughing. "Her plan to get out of a huge punishment if her lie was discovered. I would've done that if I were her."

I thought about it. Why, that little... "Son of a bitch."

She laughed and rolled onto her side, resting her weight on her elbow. "Yeah. You might have gotten played." She patted my chest, directly over my heart. "Don't worry. It's happened to the best of us."

"Not to you, I'd bet," I muttered, glowering at the ceiling. Had Rachel played me? Probably. The girl was smart like that. I didn't know whether to be pissed or impressed. "Damn her and her high IQ."

She laughed. "I don't have kids. When I do, I'm sure they'll lie to me."

"Do you want them?" I met her eyes hesitantly. "Kids, that is."

"Yeah. Of course I do." She smiled, and her whole face kind of...glowed. "I'd like at least two. I was an only child, and it sucked most of the time. I was always alone. So, maybe one of each? The boy and then the girl."

I laughed, reaching out to wrap a strand of her hair around my finger. "I'm pretty sure you don't get to pick the gender."

She lifted a shoulder. "By the time I'm ready, I might be able to." She nibbled on her lower lip. Her freckles danced over the bridge of her nose. Fucking adorable freckles. "What about you?"

"Well, I—" Her phone rang, so I stopped talking. When she didn't grab it, I raised a brow. "You going to answer that, or what? It's kind of late for casual calls."

"Not in my world, it isn't. And nope, not answering. It's my agent." She rolled her eyes. "He's called me at least ten times in the past twenty-four hours. I'll call him back later, when I'm in the mood."

"How do you know it's him?"

"Special ringtone." She bopped me on the nose. "Now answer my question."

"Which one?" I asked.

Her mouth lifted on the left side. A small half-smile. Her phone stopped ringing, and the room was silent again. "Do you want kids someday?"

"I don't know. I'm pretty fucked up. I would need a hell of a great wife to even it out so they stood half a chance of being normal."

"You're not too 'fucked up' for kids," she said, frowning at me. "You're already raising one. The teenage years are the hardest, and you're there right now. If you can do that? You can do babies."

I tugged on her hair again, the warmth in my chest spreading outward at the compliment. "You wouldn't say that if I wanted *you* to have my messed-up babies."

Her eyes went wide. The phone dinged, announcing she had a voicemail. She still didn't reach for it. "Right now? I'd run in the opposite direction. But if we were older? I'd have your messed-up babies, and I'd love them."

"Well, then…" I pulled her onto my chest. She looked down at me, her hair framing her face. "Maybe I'll come knocking on your door in ten years. I can write you a song and sing it on your doorstep, and then you'll know why I'm there. Does that sound good?"

She didn't laugh. Didn't even smile. Did she think I was serious? Hell, *was* I serious? "It sounds perfect."

The smile faded off my face. That sounded an awful lot like an actual plan or a promise. I should be freaking out right now. Running away. Telling her I was fucking around, because I had been. Or…maybe I hadn't been. It wouldn't work between us right now, but that didn't mean it couldn't in the future.

When Rachel was in college, and I was free to move… could it actually work?

"Mackenzie?" I lifted my hand, curling it around her cheek. She was so soft and sweet. So very perfect. Everything

I wasn't. A guy like me didn't deserve her. "I'm…shit, I don't know."

I wanted to tell her that I would wait for her, and ask her to wait for me. But that wasn't fair or realistic. And I wasn't any good for her. Sure, I'd be thankful for every day she gave me, knowing she could have done so much better than an asshole like me with a record and a history darker than midnight itself, but that didn't mean I'd be the best thing that ever happened to her.

But it did mean I'd very well know I didn't deserve her, so I would treat her like the fucking princess she was. Every second of every day. Could I actually get a happily-ever-after ending in my life?

"You never know, right?" she asked, breathlessly. "In a few years, we might see each other from across the room, like in the movies. We'll look at each other, locking eyes, and then in slow motion…" She leaned in closer, slow inch by slow inch. "We'll come together. And with one kiss?"

I closed my eyes. "We'll know."

"We'll just know," she agreed.

I closed the distance between us, melding our mouths together in a picture-perfect, amazing, breathtaking kiss. Right here, right now, life was sweet. But nothing that felt *this* good lasted long. For once, I wanted to believe it could, though.

Wanted to believe that a girl like her could want me, and actually be happy with me at her side indefinitely. I wanted to believe in fairy tales, unicorns, and all that crazy, shiny, happy shit that made no sense in the real world. "Mac, I should—"

Her phone rang again. It sounded different, so it wasn't her agent. She broke off the kiss and reached for it, smiling at me apologetically. "Sorry. That's my PR rep. If she's calling, it's important. Just give me a sec?"

"Sure."

I rested my hands behind my head, my mind whirling around at breakneck speeds. I was a bit of a commitment-phobe, and I wasn't going to lie about that. But with Mackenzie, this unspoken promise that wasn't really a promise felt abso-fucking-lutely right.

"He's a what?" Mackenzie said, her eyes locked on me. "No, I didn't know that. He didn't mention it. Huge shocker there, huh?" She paused, her eyes going even narrower. "Who knows?" A pause. "Well, that's just fabulous."

My heart stuttered in my chest. Oh God. This was it. She knew who I was. What I was. She must have found out that I beat the hell out of my dad, and that he'd pressed charges against me. I had a record because of it. I thought she would understand why I'd done what I'd done, but I guess I'd been wrong.

This was the beginning of the end.

And there was nothing I could do to stop it.

Mackenzie

I clutched the phone so tight my hand hurt, but I couldn't make myself relax. Just seconds before, I'd been in Austin's arms. I'd been so sure that we were going somewhere great. Somewhere with promise and hope and maybe even love. He'd been looking at me so tenderly. As if *I* mattered to him.

He'd told me things he'd never told anyone else.

I'd done the same.

And now, I found out it was all a ploy to get closer to me? To sell my pictures? All the warning signs had been there, but I'd ignored them stubbornly. God, how could I have been so freaking stupid *again*? He'd lied to me once. He'd lied to me again.

There wouldn't be a third time.

He was a photographer. A freaking paparazzi. He sold photos to tabloids. Photos I sought to avoid at all costs. Already, pictures of Austin and me in the snorkeling cove were surfacing. He hadn't wasted any time in betraying me. My PR rep said that he must have had an accomplice, because

God knows he'd been too busy blowing my mind straight into stupidity to take pictures of it all.

And I'd fallen for every single word, too. Eaten it up like candy.

"…It's on TMZ, ET, E! News. You name it, the pictures are there. And they know who he is, too. They're calling you the princess and the pauper." I heard something slam down. "Did you know what he was? Or that he had a record for kicking the snot out of his father when he was seventeen?"

I closed my eyes. That last part didn't surprise me a bit. His father deserved it and more. But the rest? Him using me for a good story? That hurt. "No, but I'll take care of it. I'll lay low until it's time to come home. Don't worry."

"This isn't something we can just wait out, Mackenzie. It's everywhere. You're not with a drummer or a frat boy this time. You're with a guy who almost went to jail." Another slam. "And on top of that, he's in the *paparazzi*. Do you have any idea what that means?"

"Yes," I said through my teeth. "I do."

I hadn't stopped watching him since Theresa called. He was looking back at me, his own face looking grim. It hurt to look at him now, knowing what I knew. I'd thought I met a guy who liked me for me. I'd obviously been wrong.

"We'll talk when you get back. I suggest leaving town early. At the very least, don't leave your hotel room until you're going to the airport. Lay low and don't be seen with him again, no matter what you do." She sighed. "The paparazzi are going to be swarming that place now. And him, too. Serves him right, the jackass."

I nodded, then realized she couldn't see me. Duh. "I'll let you know what I decide to do once I'm alone again. I need a minute."

"Oh my God. Is he there with you now?" Theresa asked, whispering as if he could hear her or something. "Do you need security to come up and assist you with removal?"

"No, I've got it." I cleared my throat. "But I'll remember

that if I do need help."

I hung up on her. My heart squeezed so tight that it hurt to breathe. My palms sweated and my legs trembled so badly I knew I would fall flat on my face if I tried to stand. I couldn't even think about moving from my spot on the bed. I was naked. Laughably, vulnerably naked…yet it didn't matter. I'd trusted him. Put myself out there. And he'd betrayed me.

Utterly, completely, heartlessly betrayed me.

"I can explain," he said, his voice soft.

"Oh, really?" I asked, covering my face. "Tell me, was it funny, knowing you fooled me?"

He pushed himself up into a seated position. "I assume you found out about my past? About me getting arrested for beating my dad into the ground?"

"Oh, yeah. I found out about that all right." I laughed, trying to hide the pain piercing my heart. "But I don't care about what you did to him. From what you told me, he deserved a beating, if not more."

He blinked at me. "If not you're not upset about that, then what's going on? If it's about me taking—"

I snorted. "You know, you're good. Better than the others. I had no idea what you were or what you were doing. None at all, and I'm good at spotting people who are only looking to sell me out." I rolled out of the bed, grabbed my robe, and closed it around myself. "How could you do that to me, Austin? After I…after we…?"

I shook my head, not bothering to finish the sentence.

"I'm so fucking confused right now." He stood up and grabbed his boxers. "Can you just tell me exactly what you're upset about so we can talk like rational adults?"

"Oh, I'm perfectly rational right now." I closed the belt of my robe so tight it hurt. Grabbing the remote, I pointed it at the TV and jammed the power button down. "*Here's* what's wrong with me."

The last channel I'd been watching had been E!, so it was easy to fill him in—but he already knew exactly what would be up there. The picture of us making out in the cove was on the screen, for the whole world to see. His hand was under the water, and both of us knew exactly what he'd been doing with that hand.

And how much I'd loved every second of it.

I turned up the volume. The annoying reporter who had always hated me was having a field day with this. "The man, Austin Murphy, was arrested for violently assaulting his father, but narrowly escaped conviction. After a failed music career and his father's police-investigated suicide, Austin returned home to raise his little sister, Rachel Murphy."

"Son of a fucking bitch," Austin growled. "They said her name."

I looked at him, for the first time wondering if I'd misjudged him. Maybe…but no. It wasn't possible. It had to be him. He'd done this. There was no other explanation.

The reporter continued. "We've been told they met in a bar in Key West, and have been seen hitting the streets ever since. He's even been spotted leaving her hotel several times. So, do this princess and pauper stand a chance at happily ever after? Knowing Mackenzie as I do…I'd vote no."

Austin glared at the TV, his entire body tense.

"What. The. Hell?" Austin snarled. "Who did this?"

"Oh, come on." I sat on the edge of the bed. "Are you really trying to tell me this wasn't you?"

"I'm not 'trying' for a damn thing." He stepped into his jeans, his arms trembling. "I didn't do this. Why the fuck would I want to put myself through this? Not to mention Rachel? Our names and family history are now plastered all over the fucking TV. You think I'd do that to her on purpose?"

God, I wanted to believe him, but I couldn't. I'd already fallen for his lies once. I couldn't do it again. "Maybe if the price was right. Tell me, was it right?"

He froze, his pants half on. "You know what? Fuck you."

"No, fuck you." I threw my shirt at him. It bounced off his head painlessly. I wanted to do damage. As much damage as he'd done to me. "You screwed me over for what? A few bucks?" I threw my underwear at him. I needed something harder, damn it. "Was it worth a couple of dinners out at a nice restaurant?"

He totally ignored my missiles. Didn't even flinch at them. But his face turned red, and he buckled his pants with jerky motions. "If I had sold your photos, and my story with it, then I'd have made enough to put food on the table and a roof over our heads for months. Do you have any idea how much of a relief it would be for a guy who struggles to support a teenager every fucking day? You have no idea what the real world is like."

I swallowed hard. God, he sounded so sincere. Could he really be that good of an actor? Or maybe he was innocent in this. But the mere idea seemed like way too much wishful thinking on my part. "You're telling me it wasn't you who leaked this story and photo?"

"Yes, and it's the fucking truth. Don't you think if it was me, they'd have more information? They know nothing about us. All they have is my old criminal file and a fucking picture. One I clearly didn't take, since I'm in it." He gestured to the TV. "Or did you forget that tiny fact?"

I lifted a shoulder, trying to hang on to my skepticism. It was harder than you'd think when faced with such righteous anger. "You could have had a partner."

"I don't." He met my eyes, the haunting look in them hurting me. "I didn't *do* this to you, Mackenzie."

I didn't know what to think. I mean, he seemed as if he was telling me the truth, but I wanted to believe him so badly that I couldn't trust my judgment. I'd be an idiot if I did. He'd lied to me. Hidden his identity. Taken pictures and sold them for a living. But despite every reason not to believe in him…

I was fairly certain he was telling me the truth. I *really* was.

"I believe you," I said, dropping my head in defeat. "God help me, but I do. Why didn't you tell me what you did for a living in the first place?"

He didn't react to my words at all, outwardly. "Why would I? My previous side job had nothing to do with us. I wasn't going to use you or sell photos, so it didn't seem important for me to fess up. You want the dirty, tawdry confession? Fine. Back when I lived in L.A., I used to occasionally sell pictures of celebrities when I was low on cash. It's how I supported myself when I looked for a record label to sign me. But I've never fucked one to get an inside scoop, and I haven't sold a goddamn picture since I've been Rachel's guardian. That's the truth, and I'm leaving now."

He headed for the door, and I chased after him, my heart pounding so hard it hurt. I couldn't let him walk away angry. I couldn't let him…I couldn't let him leave me.

"I'm *so* sorry." I grabbed his arm by the elbow and he stopped walking. He could easily shake me off, but he didn't. "I'm sorry I jumped to conclusions. Sorry I assumed you'd done this, but it's happened to me before, and I just…I panicked. That's all. I'm sorry."

His jaw flexed. "I know you've been betrayed before, Mac." He looked toward the door. "And apology accepted, but you have to let go. I need to leave."

I swallowed hard, letting my hand drop back to my side, even though it went against every nerve in my body. "Are you going home to check on Rachel?"

His phone vibrated. "Yeah. That's probably her right now."

"Okay." I nodded, watching as he checked his messages. His sister came first. That made complete sense. "When you've got that squared away, you can come back here so we can figure out what comes next. Hey, you can bring her with you, if you want. And then we can—"

"*Stop*," he said, his voice hard.

I blinked at him, not sure what to do next. "Okay. What's up?"

"I'm not coming back."

My throat ached, but I refused to let the sob trying to escape come loose. Not now. Not in front of him. "You're not?"

"No, I'm not. You immediately assumed it was me who sold you out, without even *asking* me." He held his arms out to his sides. "You don't trust me. That's fine. I can accept that. But let me tell you a little something about myself: I'm not a bullshitter. I don't have the patience for it. It's why I'm still single—I don't have the tolerance for this relationship shit. I didn't fucking *do* it, Mac."

"I know." I bit down on my lower lip. I didn't know what to think. Or do. Or say. So I settled for, "I already told you I believe you. And I'm sorry I—"

He started for the door. "I know you're sorry, and so am I. I'm sorry that this didn't work out, but we both knew it wouldn't, didn't we?"

"Austin, *please*. Don't go." I covered my face with my hands, but watched him through my fingers. I couldn't look away from the anger in his eyes. "I'm sorry I assumed it was you without asking. It won't happen again."

For a second, I thought he might have changed his mind. His face softened, and he took a step toward me. But then...he stopped. It all stopped. "I know it won't."

Slowly, my heart wrenching, I lowered my hands. "W-What are you saying?"

He eyed me. "It's time to say goodbye, Mac. I'm done. *We're* done." He grabbed his shirt and turned it right side out. "That was always our plan, right? That we would walk away from each other at the end of the week?"

My heart twisted even tighter, making a small gasp escape my lips. He was walking away from me because I hadn't trusted him. I knew it. He knew it.

"What if we wait this storm out?" I held out my hands. "See what happens after this all blows over? Right before my phone rang, we were talking about the future."

There wasn't a trace of tenderness visible in his eyes. He looked at me as if I was already a part of his past, and to him? I probably was. "It doesn't matter what we were talking about. The moment passed. And we already know what happens. You

110

leave. I stay."

"It doesn't have to be this way," I said, my heart shattering into thousands of shards. "Please don't go. I don't want you to go."

For a second, I thought I'd gotten through to him. His blue eyes softened, and he looked as if he was going to say something to me. Something good. But then he backed away from me, shaking his head slowly. "I don't have a choice anymore."

"Austin..." I'd chosen to jump to conclusions about who had sold that picture to the paparazzi, and now I was paying the consequences. Would anyone else in my situation have reacted any differently? I wasn't sure. "There's always a choice. I chose to make the wrong assumptions, and now you're choosing to leave."

He shook his head. "There's only one choice for me. I don't need the paparazzi watching me when I pick up Rachel from school. Don't need them watching me at all. Rachel deserves better than having her whole life plastered on the TV for America's entertainment."

And I'd done that to them. I'd ruined their privacy. Taken it all away. All because he'd dared to be seen with me. This was my world. It didn't have to be his. "You're right, of course. I'm sorry for doing this to you."

"I don't want this life." He met my eyes. "And I don't want you."

I flinched. I couldn't help it. "That was harsh."

"Yeah, well, life is harsh sometimes." He lifted his shoulder. "You live in the limelight, and you like it. But I don't, and I won't. This thing we have going on between us? It won't work. It never could have."

"I...I understand," I said, my voice breaking along with my heart. He was a normal guy, and I wasn't a normal girl. Why I would have ever thought it could have worked out between us was beyond me. That had been the foolish thinking of a foolish girl. I wouldn't be her anymore. "But before you go, please know that I didn't mean to hurt you. I just...I don't know. I just reacted."

"Yeah. And now I am, too." He reached out and brushed his hand across my jaw, then let go of me. I almost wondered if I'd imagined the whole thing. He yanked his shirt over his head. "We're not meant to be."

I fisted my hands even tighter. I'd been so angry at him earlier, but now he was breaking my heart. How was that even possible? We barely knew each other. We'd only spent a few days together, yet knowing he was done with me hurt.

He could walk away so easily, as if nothing about us mattered, yet I felt as if he was ripping out my heart. How was this fair? Whoever had written that song about a heart not breaking evenly was *so* right.

"You're right. This was a fling and nothing more," I said, my voice hollow. He didn't need to know how much this hurt. Didn't need to know anything more about me than he already did. "We agreed on a few days, and that's what we got. It was fun."

"Right." He swallowed so hard I could see his Adam's apple bob up and down. "Goodbye, Mac. Good luck with... everything."

I managed to offer him a tight smile. "Yeah. You too."

He opened the door, hesitating at the threshold. I held my breath, waiting for him to take away all the pain. To go back to what we'd been saying before my publicist called. Anything besides this cold, hard reality that was being shoved down my throat.

I didn't want it. Didn't want this.

"Austin..." I said, my voice trailing off. There was so much I wanted to say, but none of it seemed fitting. None of it seemed right. I could write the perfect line in a song, or create the perfect string of chords, but when it came to something that *mattered*, I came up dry. Freaking son of a bitch. "I...I..."

His hand flexed on the knob. "Yeah. I know."

He walked through the door and closed it behind him, the sound loud and so final in the empty room. I sank to the couch, my legs no longer supporting me. Maybe if I had asked him if he'd betrayed me before going off the handle, this fight would have ended differently. Or maybe if his sister's name hadn't been dragged into the mud, he would have given us a chance.

But I hadn't. And he hadn't. And she had been.

It was over, and I was alone again. This is what I'd wanted, right? I'd wanted to lose my virginity and then walk away from the guy I chose. No strings. No feelings.

I guess it was too late for either of those things.

CHAPTER *Thirteen*

Austin

$\mathcal{I}$ swiped the rag across the bar and checked the clock. I only had about thirty minutes until I had to go up on stage, and I could barely get a breath in my lungs, let alone hold a note. All night long, girls had been flirting with me. I was used to that, but this time it was different.

They were pushy. Didn't take a cold shoulder for a no. And it had everything to do with the fact that I'd been in photos with Mackenzie. It was almost as if they thought if they fucked me, they had a connection to her or some shit like that. It was fucked up and stupid. And I was done.

If one more girl sprawled across my bar and tried to get my attention…

I hadn't even finished the thought before a girl raised her hand and lay across my bar. I was about to tell her to stick her hand where the sun don't shine, but then I focused on her face.

I recognized her. It was one of Mac's friends. Her other friend was here, too. The one who had been with flirting with the dude who looked familiar.

The only one missing was my girl. Not that she was my girl anymore.

What had she done all day today? Had she left after our fight last night? Is that why she wasn't here? Or was she hiding from the cameras? I was dying to know.

Maybe now I'd find out, through the help of her friend.

I forced a smile, not sure what I'd be getting from her. Did she hate me, like Mac probably did? Maybe she would tell me to go to hell and slap me. I probably deserved it for something I did in my lifetime, I'm sure. "Quinn, right? Mac's friend?"

"Yes! Austin, right?"

So she knew my name. That made me happy for some reason. But if Mac had told her about me, it had probably been all the bad shit. "You got it."

"Listen, I haven't been able to reach Mac. She okay?"

My heart clenched tight, but I nodded. "Yeah. She's been holed up in her room for a bit."

Or maybe she was gone. How the fuck should I know when we weren't speaking? And shouldn't Mac's friend know all about it by now?

Wait a second. Was it possible she didn't know what had happened between us? What had happened with TMZ and pretty much every other news channel in America? I didn't think it was possible for her to miss it, but from the looks of it, she'd been hanging with some pretty heavy drinkers all week.

Her eyes lit up. "Got it. Can you just tell her to call me when she's got a chance? I'm not at the hotel—I'm staying somewhere else tonight, so I don't want her to worry if she comes to my door."

I frowned. "With that guy?" I motioned toward the loud assholes at the end of my bar. They were getting louder by the second, tossing some small scrap of cloth amongst themselves. "I may have to cut them off. Never went through so much tequila in my life, and they get a little over the top when they get together."

She flushed. "I think that's a good idea. But don't tell them I confirmed."

I leaned in really far so I could whisper in her ear. "Smart girl. Thanks for the heads-up."

She grinned. "Welcome."

Should I tell her about the paparazzi? She seemed nice enough, and maybe Mac hadn't told her friends yet. Maybe she was all alone and scared and upset, trying to keep the truth from them so they could enjoy their vacations, even if she couldn't. Shit. That was totally something she would do. "Listen, Quinn. About Mac."

She went still. "Is she okay?"

I shifted on my feet. "There was some trouble. Paps found out about us. She needs you."

She cursed and then her eyes narrowed. Right on time— the suspicion I'd been expecting all along. "Was it you?"

I glared right back at her. "Fuck no. Believe what you want. I don't need this shit."

I turned away, but she grabbed my wrist, so I stopped out of respect. It's not as if she could have held me back even if she threw her weight into it. "I'm sorry. I—I believe you. Is she at the hotel?"

Wait. What? She believed me. Impossible. "Yeah. Surrounded by the press. We were on TMZ. Fucking shit."

"Crap. Okay, I'm heading over there now to check on her."

I had to ask. "Why do you believe me?"

She looked at me, saying nothing at first. "Don't know. Just do."

"Thanks. Wait here." I ran back to the mixing station and grabbed a styrofoam cup before throwing together a drink for her. "Here. It's a Sex on the Beach. Take one for the road. Mac said it's your signature drink."

"Thanks."

I lowered my voice. "Thanks for believing me."

She nodded and left, and I watched her go. My boss motioned me up to the stage, and I made quick work of readying myself in the back room. The whole time I changed, I thought about Mac. Could I do this? Could I let her walk away?

I didn't know. All I knew was I was supposed to be out on stage, and I wasn't ready. And when I stumbled out there, I totally lost my mind. I couldn't fucking believe this shit. After years of being in the shadows, of no one knowing who the hell I was and me being perfectly content for it to stay that way…

I had a full house and the paparazzi at my nine o'clock show. I climbed up on the small stage, my acoustic guitar in my hands, and settled down on the stool mid-stage. The cheap colored lights at the edge of the stage lit up, and I took a steadying breath.

Ready or not, it was show time.

I scanned the crowd. People were packed into the bar like sardines in a can, and they were all watching *me*. They were smiling and cheering as if I was this mega-fucking superstar. I wasn't.

And all throughout my half-hour segment, they kept trying to sing along, even though they didn't know any of my damn songs. They acted like groupies. All because I'd been caught with my fingers inside Mackenzie Forbes. It didn't seem fair. And if Mackenzie saw this, it would only make her think I'd used her for fame and fortune all over again.

The funny thing was, I didn't even want either one. Ever since I left L.A., singing was something I did for *me*. I didn't do it for recognition or even money. I'd given up on that dream long ago. I liked it. It made me happy—so I did it.

End of story.

Half an hour later, I took a breath and finished my last song. I strummed my pick across the strings, playing a few chords, and let myself get lost in the music.

"It's something you feel all the way through… Love isn't something you can buy or steal… It's something you have to fight

117

to feel… And I never have, until you."

The crowd broke out in applause, and I swallowed hard. I'd just finished the song I'd written for Mackenzie this morning. I'd been restless ever since I'd walked away from her yesterday. Sure, it had always been the plan. To end things when the time came. It just came a little earlier than we'd been planning.

Maybe that's why it was killing me so fucking much.

I took off my guitar and bowed to the crowd. "Thank you for coming out."

Flashes blinded me, and people shouted questions. Questions they had no right asking. I vowed to never take another picture of a celebrity ever again. This was ridiculous. Funny, I'd never thought a few pictures were a big deal before now.

"Are you going to Mackenzie's after this?"

"Is Mackenzie backstage?"

"Just how serious are you two?"

"Why did you almost kill your father?"

"What can you tell us about your shady past?"

I ignored them all, walking off the stage without another word. Asshats. I knew that any other artist would be happy with the new attention. But instead, I was fucking miserable because I already missed her. It was time I admitted it to myself, and maybe to her, too.

I'd been wrong to throw her aside, just as she'd been wrong to assume I'd been the one to sell her out. She'd touched me in ways no one else ever had. She'd made me open my heart. Open my past. Hope for the future. But was that enough for us to make something of ourselves, despite all the hardships we'd be facing? She was leaving. Going back to college.

I was here, and would always be here. At least until Rachel grew up.

My phone buzzed. Was that her? Mackenzie? She hadn't tried to contact me since last night, but then again, I hadn't tried to contact her either. I pulled out my phone, releasing a sigh when I saw it was a text from Rachel. *You going to see*

Mackenzie behind my back again?

I rolled my eyes and typed back. *No.*

She would never forgive me for not telling her I was involved with her role model. Even though I'd been upset on her behalf, she hadn't cared about her past being aired like dirty laundry. She'd just been angry at me for not telling her about it.

But it hadn't exactly been common knowledge...until it had been. What had she expected me to do? Blurt it out for all to hear? Not happening.

My phone buzzed again. *Well, stuck at home since I'm grounded. So feel free to...do whatever you do when I'm not with you. Mrs. Greer can come over again.*

I chuckled. *I cry until I return to your arms.*

Haha. So funny. Tell Mackenzie she's invited over for pizza sometime. I'd love to meet her.

I shook my head. *It would be too much of a mess. The whole world would know our business. I can't do that to you.*

They already know our history. Why stop now? You have my blessing, bro. Go for it. Don't let fear stop you.

I started to say it didn't matter because I wouldn't be seeing Mackenzie again anyway, but then I froze. *You know what? I'll go see her after all.*

I'll let Mrs. Greer know!

I grinned, feeling freer than I'd felt in a long damn time. *Love ya.*

Love you too.

After shooting a quick text to Mrs. Greer to confirm she was indeed going over to sit with Rachel, I shoved my phone into my pocket. Normally I'd let her stay home alone, but after what she'd tried to pull off, I didn't trust her to stay put just yet. It was time to try to get Mac back in my arms, and it was now or never. I didn't know exactly what I wanted to say yet, but I knew I had to see her.

Hopefully the words would come to me before I got there. I changed clothes, hoping that would throw off the paparazzi. After trading my green shirt for a black one and a pair of matching jeans, I tugged a Redskins hat low over my head and strolled out of the bar whistling. I tried to look as normal and laid back as possible, and it must've worked.

I walked right past the waiting photographers without them noticing.

"She's leaving on Saturday. I'm going to camp out at the airport after I get another picture of her latest Romeo," a blond photographer said, adjusting his camera lenses. "She's got horrible taste in men lately."

I wanted to flip him off and say, "Kiss my ass, fucker," but I wanted to go talk to Mackenzie even more. So I bit my tongue and strolled right under their noses. She was leaving soon. I knew that, but hearing it made it all the more…final. Damn it all to hell.

I didn't want to let her go.

Mackenzie

I opened the door at the knock, half expecting to find Austin in the hallway again, just like Tuesday night. Before it all went to hell. But I should have known it wasn't going to be him. Austin never would have gotten past the security I'd been forced to call after the big reveal. My most loyal guard, Harry, was pissed.

And he wouldn't be afraid to show it.

It was Quinn, and she looked like she'd been crying for hours. Last I'd heard, she was at the bar with her guy and had been happy as a clam. What could have happened between now and then to make her so upset? Whatever it was, or whoever had caused it, I was going to kill them.

I pulled her into my arms for a hug. "Oh my God, are you okay?"

Quinn nodded shakily. "Yeah. I think. What the hell is going on, sweetie? Why didn't you tell me about getting busted by the pap yesterday?"

I stepped to the side and motioned her in, but then decided to haul her in when she didn't move fast enough. This was not a conversation I wanted to have in the hallway. I'd been hiding out in my room since the big fight with Austin. No one needed to know how much of a wreck I was right now. No one needed to know I was nursing a broken heart.

But if I stood in the hallway talking about it, they might hear about it.

I didn't want to risk being seen now, after all the lengths I went through to remain unseen. America would love seeing me broken-hearted, I'm sure. Seeing me down in the dumps with frizzy hair and no makeup. But they wouldn't get to if I had my way.

I tried to play it off with a shrug. Quinn was supposed to be out having fun, not worrying about my pathetic love life. "I couldn't deal. I wanted you to have a nice vacation and not worry about me."

"He didn't. Austin didn't leak the news."

"I know. I mean, I thought he did at first, but then I realized I was wrong. It was too late." I blinked back the tears trying to escape. "How did you know about it?"

She lifted her chin. "Because it was me."

I laughed. "Really funny."

"I'm not kidding. I didn't actually do it, but I might as well have." She sat down on the couch and covered her face with her hands. "I told James about you. Told him I was here with you. I trusted him, and his friend...he did it."

I sat down beside her and rubbed her back. "James told them?"

"No. James's buddy. Dickhead Adam." She uncovered her face. "He must have been eavesdropping...or maybe James told him. I don't even know."

I swallowed hard. The news didn't surprise me at all. I already knew Austin was innocent, so it had to be someone, right? It happened to be some douche I'd never met. "It's okay.

That's not your fault."

Quinn shook her head. "But it is. I told James. If I hadn't told him, then you'd—"

"I'd still be me, and chances are? Someone else would have figured it out," I said matter-of-factly. "It was only a matter of time, really. The truth is, I'm not even upset about being found out. I'm upset with how I reacted to it. I shouldn't have assumed it was Austin. If I hadn't, maybe he would have stayed with me instead of leaving. But it's too late now."

"Mac…" She hugged me close, and I smiled as she kissed my cheek. "You're too good to me, you know that?"

"Please. I'm not good enough." I let go of her. "You didn't do anything to be ashamed of. All you did was trust a boy…"

"And look where that got me."

I sighed. "The three of us made a mess of things down here, didn't we? What happened to carefree sex and fun? Wasn't that what I ordered us all to find?"

"I don't know." She shrugged, but didn't laugh like I expected her to. "Maybe the two don't go hand in hand."

I got up and cracked open the bottle of wine I'd ordered this morning. "I think we need this, and you're going to tell me everything that happened in detail, instead of the bits and pieces I've gotten over texts the past few days. Deal?"

Quinn finally cracked a smile. "I think I can agree to that."

Austin

I'd done it. I'd walked to her hotel, and now I just needed to go in and make her listen to me. I stopped walking and looked up toward her floor. Was she still there? Judging from the paparazzi parked outside of it, I'd say yes. I took a deep breath and walked through the doors, keeping my head down. No one stopped me.

Was I actually doing this? Going back after I'd said goodbye?

"Excuse me." Someone stopped in my path before I could make it to the front desk. "Key, please."

"Uh…" I blinked at the huge fucker in front of me. Seriously, his arms were like barrels. He could probably bench-press me without breaking a sweat. "I don't have one."

He rocked back on his heels. "Then you can turn around and walk right back out those doors. No one gets in without a key or clearance from me."

"I'm here to see a friend," I said, lifting my head to look at the dude. He had on a security shirt and had pepper spray on his hip. He was big, but I'd bet a million bucks I was faster. If I ducked under his arm, I might make it to the elevator before he killed me. "Mackenzie Forbes. You're guarding her, I assume?"

He crossed his arms. "Is she expecting you?"

"No. I was trying to surprise her."

"Yeah, well, that ain't happening on my watch. You gotta be approved before you ride to her room, or you need to prove you're a guest here," he said, lifting a brow. "Which I already know you're not."

I glared at him. Huge or not, he was in my way. I should have known Mac would call in the guards after everyone learned her location. It only made sense. Actually, I was surprised that she hadn't left already.

"I need to talk to her, and you're not stopping me. I've been kicked on or punched my whole fucking life just for being alive." I shrugged. "You're not all that scary to a guy like me."

"Be that as it may, you need to join the rest of the scum out there before we test that theory." He cocked his head toward the paparazzi. "They are your friends, right, Mr. Murphy?"

"No, they're not." I pulled out my phone. "I assume you know her, right?"

"You could say that, yes. I watch out for men like you in Chicago. They all know not to mess with me. Maybe you need to learn that lesson, too." He eyed me and moved his fingers. His wedding band caught the light. "I've been her guard for three years, and I don't take kindly to little punks like you

123

hurting her."

I hadn't hurt her. Okay. Maybe I had. But she'd hurt me, too. "Then you'll recognize her voice." I dialed her number, holding my breath and praying she answered.

It rang once, twice, three times. Then, she finally picked up. "What do you want, Austin?" She sounded tired. Maybe she'd been up all night, too. "I'm not in the mood to fight with you. I have to pack."

I closed my eyes. Shit, even her voice made me more relaxed than the three beers I'd had before I got on the stage. "When are you leaving? Tomorrow or Saturday?"

She sighed. "Saturday."

I'd been wrong. She wasn't leaving tomorrow. We had a whole day together still—if I managed to get her to forgive me, that is. "I need to talk to you."

"Fine." She sighed. "Talk."

"I want to do it in person." I clutched the phone tight, opening my eyes and watching her guard cautiously. He looked ready to pummel me into the tile at a moment's notice. I'd bet he would like it, too. "I can't get through your human door, though."

"What do you want to say that can't be said over the phone?"

"Please." I shifted on my feet, eyeing the elevator. If she didn't get her guard to let me through, I was running for it full speed ahead. It would only get me to the floor under hers without someone to swipe me up there, but it was better than nothing. "I'm begging you, Mac."

Silence. "Put Harry on."

I handed Harry the phone. "She wants to talk to you."

Harry lifted the phone to his ear. "Yes, miss?" A nod. "All right." He hung up and handed me the phone. He cracked his knuckles and stepped in my path. "She said to get rid of you with as much force as necessary."

I swallowed hard and lifted my chin. Un-fucking-believable. She refused to let me talk to her? Bullshit. She

124

would have to remove me forcibly and make a scene if she wanted to play that way. "Then do it. I'm not leaving on my own accord until I talk to her, no matter how many times you crack your knuckles."

Harry laughed, throwing his head back. Holy shitballs. His laugh was even deeper than his voice. "I'm messing with you. She said to let you through without hurting you."

I released the breath I'd been holding. "Oh. Good."

"Go on, before I change my mind." He moved aside, watching me with those unflinching brown eyes the whole time. "And don't make her cry again, or you'll answer to me."

She'd been crying? Well, shit. I hadn't meant to hurt her.

He walked me to the elevator and swiped his card, allowing me to ride up to the top without an escort. The whole way up, my knees were wobbling and my hands were sweating. I knew this was my only chance to make my point. My only chance to get a happy ending with her. And, man, I needed that chance.

That's what I had to tell her. She needed to know, no matter how she felt about me, she had to know *I* needed *her*. That I didn't want her to go. That I wasn't ready to call it quits, no matter what I'd said yesterday during our fight.

I knocked on the door, my heart racing faster than a fucking NASCAR racecar. I stood there, staring at the wood door. When it opened, my gaze fell on her flushed cheeks and messy hair. She didn't have on any makeup, and she wore a cowboy hat, a pair of jean shorts, a plaid shirt, and cowboy boots.

She'd never looked more gorgeous.

"Hi," I said.

She blinked at me. "Hi."

"Why are you wearing a hat?"

She pulled it off and tossed it behind her. "I was about to leave."

"Oh. Well, we need to talk." She didn't step out of the way, but she didn't close the door in my face either. "Can I come in?"

125

"I don't know if that's a good idea," she said, nibbling on her bottom lip.

"I was wrong last night." I leaned on the doorjamb, holding her gaze. "Please let me in?"

For a second I thought she would say no. Her gaze dipped low, skimming over my ink and then going even lower. By the time her green eyes met mine again, I was sure she'd shut the door in my face. But then she stepped back, motioning me inside. "Look, I'm—"

"Wait. Let me talk first." I walked inside, closing the door. I tossed my phone on the table out of habit. It was time to man up and be completely honest. To tell her how I felt. For better or worse, she needed to know. "I wrote you a song, and I was going to sing it to you like I said I would last night, but I changed my mind. Instead, I'm going to tell you this: I want to love you."

CHAPTER
Fourteen

Mackenzie

I blinked at Austin, doubting my hearing. Had he just told me he wanted to love me? Who said something like that? You either loved someone or you didn't. You didn't want to *try* to love someone or have to guess at it.

It just happened—at least, I think that's how it worked.

And I still couldn't believe he was here. I'd been getting ready to go to the bar to find him, despite the media frenzy it would cause, because I couldn't leave without letting him know how I felt. I'd never felt so deeply for a guy before. He'd changed me, for the better, and I'd wanted to let him know that.

But then *he* had called *me*.

"Wait. What?" I rubbed my eyes, wondering if I'd dozed off or something. "What are you trying to say?"

"I don't know." He yanked on his collar. "Fuck."

He paced in front of me, restless energy rolling off of him with each step. He wore a Redskins hat, a black T-shirt, and jeans paired with a pair of dark blue kicks. In other words, he looked like the Austin I'd come to know and care about.

But…he'd walked away from me yesterday. He'd been the one ready to throw it all away. He'd been the one who left. Now he was here, talking about wanting to love me? "I don't understand," I said, shaking my head. "Why do you *want* to love me?"

"Let me start over. I had all these people at my show tonight. Tons, actually. And I sang a new song. A song I wrote after I walked away yesterday. I couldn't sleep last night. Couldn't rest. Couldn't stop thinking about what we could have been." He dragged his hands down his face. "I know it's crazy, and I know we had a rough start. But I can't shake the feeling that you're the one. And I'll be damned if I'll let you be the one who got away, too."

I let out a weird, strangled sound. He didn't need to say another word. I was his if he wanted me. No questions asked. No hesitation. I was *in*. "Austin…"

"I know I hurt you." He dropped his hands and approached me, his eyes open and vulnerable and so beautifully blue that it hurt to look at him. He stopped directly in front of me. "I know thinking we can make this work is fucking stupid and impetuous—some might even call it a daydream. But I can't let you go without a fight. I think, if you let me, I could love you so damn good. I could make you happy, and you'll save me from myself. Just say yes. Just give me another chance."

"Yes. So much yes."

Before I could say another word, he closed his hands around my shoulders and kissed me, his mouth fitting mine perfectly. I gripped his biceps, holding on tight so he'd stay right where he was. I didn't want to lose him again.

His words rang in my head. He wanted to love me? Really love me? How could I say no to that, when I felt the same way about him? We might not have known each other for long, but he knew more about me than most of the people in my life.

And I knew him, too.

He broke off the kiss, gasping for air. "Really? You'll give us a shot?"

"Heck yeah. I can't imagine *not* giving us a shot, Austin." He went for my mouth again, but I gave him my cheek. "Wait. I'm so sorry for flying off the handle like that."

"I know." He kissed my forehead. "We both said things we shouldn't have last night, but what matters is we're here now. We're committed to one another now, and that's all that we need. Together, we can make this work. I know it."

I nodded. "I agree completely. But I have to tell you something. I know who actually did it."

He tensed. "Who was it? I'll kick his fucking ass."

"One of Quinn's new guy's so-called friends." I shrugged. "He heard her talking about me and then followed us out to the cove."

"Fucker."

I nodded. "Yeah. I was about to come to your bar and see if you could maybe give me another chance. That's why I was wearing the hat. I was going to try to sneak out the back."

A smiled played at his mouth. "You were going to come to me?"

"I was." I cupped his face, resting my thumb over his chin dimple. "I'll always come for you, no matter what."

He hugged me tight. "I'm so fucking happy right now. I was scared you'd have left already, and that I'd never see you again. Why haven't you left?"

She lifted a shoulder. "It's not Quinn's and Cassie's fault that someone sold me out. Why punish them by making them leave early? If I had left, they would have insisted on coming with me for support. There's no doubt about it, and I didn't want to ruin their vacation because I'd been found out by a dick with a camera."

"*Mac*." He shook his head and a smile slowly spread across his face. "You're fucking amazing. You know that, right?"

I placed my hands on his chest. He tried to kiss me again, but I avoided his mouth. I wanted that kiss, and I would gladly accept it, but there were some things that had to be said first. "Wait. Not yet. You had your turn to talk, so now it's my turn."

"Fine." He rested his forehead on mine. "If you say something that breaks what little heart I have left, I'm still not leaving. I'm going to make you love me, even if it takes fifty years."

I let out a little laugh. "I highly doubt it'll take that long." I licked my lips, watching as his eyes went wide. "God, I missed you so much. It's only been less than a day, but it felt like a freaking year without you here. Did it feel the same for you?"

"Like ages and ages of despair." He lifted his face to the ceiling, grinning wide. "And now I'm in fucking heaven. We can do this. We'll make it work. I know you have to go back to college, but we can do long distance. There's FaceTime and email and texts—"

"Nope." I pressed my fingers to his mouth, cutting off his torrent. "We don't have to do that. Either you and Rachel can come with me, or I'll transfer down here."

The smile I loved so much faded away. "I can't make Rachel move. I promised her she could graduate with her friends, and I'm not breaking any more promises to her." He cupped my face, his solemn eyes on me. "And I can't make you change your college just for me. I would never ask that of you."

I held on to his forearms. "I respect that about you, that you won't ask me to change my whole life for you. But I think you're going to become the biggest thing in my life, Austin. I can feel it. Here." I let go of him and pressed a hand to his heart. It sped up under my touch. "How about this for a compromise? I'll finish up the school year in Chicago. But then, if we're still feeling this way? If we're still serious about us? I'm coming down here, to be with you."

He laid his hand over mine, holding it even closer to his chest. "If we feel this way, and I have no doubt we will, then I agree with your plan. I just don't want you to rush through these decisions."

"I'm not rushing through anything." I grinned up at him. "But this is us, and I know it's real. The way you make me feel…I've been singing about it for years. I never believed it was real. Never believed in this."

"And now you do?" he asked, tilting my face up to his. His lips hovered over mine, so close and yet not close enough. "Is that what you're saying?"

"Now I do, because of you."

He kissed me again, his hands roaming. Desire and need surged through my body, but it was so much more than that. There was a deeper emotion tied to it. One that I suspected would one day become love.

I hoped I never got used to the way he made me feel. Or of the way he made my whole body tingle, as he ran his calloused hands over me. The way he stole my breath away, without even trying. This was what I sang about. This was the thing of songs, poems, and books. This just might be love already.

He pressed me back against the wall, melding his body against mine with a groan. I could feel his erection pressing against me. And all those muscles…

God, I needed him so bad.

He ended the kiss, trailing his mouth down my neck. When he nipped the skin at the base of my neck, I shuddered and raked my nails down his back. His hands fell on my shorts, ripping them open, and I undid his pants. No words were needed. We'd already said them. This was all we needed now.

Each other.

My shorts fell to the floor, and I kicked out of them. My boots were still on, but who gave a damn? All that mattered was him, inside of me. He stepped out of his pants and shoes, then peeled off his gray boxer briefs. When he dropped to his knees, I gulped in a breath of air. "*Austin*."

"You look so fucking perfect," he said.

He ripped open a condom packet, his eyes on me the whole time. Once he finished putting it on, he ran his fingers over the small patch of curls above my core, and I shivered. When he slid his hand under my left leg, lifting it and looping it over his shoulder, I knew I was a goner. "Hurry. *Please*."

He growled. "Hold on tight, sweetheart."

"Gladly." I nodded frantically. "As long as you want me to. Forever."

His eyes darkened, and then he was on me. I dug my nails in his shoulders, holding on as he closed his mouth over me, flicking his tongue over my clit. My entire body came to life, all the nerves centering on that one spot within me.

The spot he brought to life with each roll of his tongue. I dropped my head back against the wall, crying out. He pressed even closer, tasting me with such abandon that I could barely stand it. The pleasure was so freaking intense it might break me.

"I...oh my God," I moaned, squeezing my eyes shut. "*Yes*."

Everything broke inside me. My control. My restraint. Everything.

I collapsed against the wall, thankful for the support. If not for his hands on me, I would have fallen to a puddle on the floor. He stood up, lifted me higher, positioned himself at my entry, and kissed me. I tasted myself on his tongue, which was more erotic than you could ever have possibly imagined it would be.

And so incredibly hot.

He thrust inside, hard and deep. I cried out, digging my nails into his back, and bit down on his shoulder. "Fuck, Mac."

He moved inside me, supporting my weight with his hands under my ass. The wall scraped my back, and I'd probably regret this tomorrow, but it was *so* worth it. He pulled out and then drove back in, over and over again, raising me higher and higher.

When he pressed me harder against the wall, his hand closing on my breast and squeezing hard, I lost all control. My nails raked over him, anywhere I could, and I screamed out things I didn't fully understand. It was rough, hard, and frantic…yet somehow it still managed to be so freaking meaningful it brought me to tears.

I bit down on my lip, my whole body going numb as I came again, the world fading to black. He groaned and thrust inside me one more time, shuddering and dropping his head against the wall. The only sound in the room was our breathing, harsh and laborious.

It was perfect.

"Fuck," he muttered, lifting his head and looking down at me with a furrowed brow. "Are you okay? I kind of lost control there at the end."

"It was perfect." I kissed him, soft and tender. "Absolutely perfect. Tell me, how am I supposed to leave after that?"

He grinned, his blue eyes blazing with happiness. "Fuck if I know."

"This last quarter better pass fast," I mumbled, holding onto him as tightly as I could. "I don't want to go back to Chicago. It's cold and snowy there, and there's no you. I'd rather just stay here with you."

"We can't do that yet. You need time to clear your head. Time to make sure it's what you really want." He kissed the tip of my nose. "You can't think clearly when I'm here asking you to try to fall in love with me. But I'll be here waiting for you when the quarter is over, that much I can promise."

"I don't *need* to go to college, you know. I just did it because I needed something to do besides music. I had nothing else to focus on." I rubbed my nose into his shoulder, inhaling his scent. "I could focus on you. It would be a heck of a lot more fun."

He snorted. "Tempting, but nope. I'm not derailing your life like that. I'm not a subject you can get a degree in. College…or no Austin."

"Well, that's not fair. *You* aren't going to college."

He shrugged. "I wasn't when we met either. Non-negotiable, sweetheart. I'll give you anything you want, but not that. You need to see it through. I won't be the one who stops

133

you or holds you back."

He kissed me, then stepped away, slowly letting my feet hit the ground again. I winced. Man, my legs hurt. Not to mention my back. "But—"

"No buts." He moved out of my reach, watching me from under those lashes that most women would kill to have. "I want to lift you up, not drag you down. Once the school year is over, we talk. Until then?" He crossed his arms. "I won't budge on my stance. Not this time."

"You're bossy," I said, pouting.

"I know. You like me that way," he said, shooting me a cocky grin.

"Psh." But he was right about everything. I'd come this far. I couldn't walk away from it all. And, darn it, I did like his cockiness. It was freaking hot. "Fine. But I'm coming down a lot. Like, as much as possible."

"That's acceptable." He yanked me into his arms.

"Good," I said, burying my face in his chest. "I can't imagine not being with you, even after this short of a time. This is crazy, isn't it?"

"Certifiably insane. Oh, and you are invited to my house for pizza tomorrow." He twisted his lips. "Rachel wants to meet you, officially."

I grinned, excited to meet the girl I'd heard so much about. "I'd love to come over. She doesn't hate me for dragging her into the spotlight?"

"Hell no. She loves you too much for that." He kissed the top of my head, but his fingers tightened on me. "Just so you know, my house is small. Like, ridiculously so. I bought it with what little money I could scrape together when I came back, and I'll be paying the mortgage on it till I die, more than likely. We don't have a lot of land or—"

I kissed him, cutting him off. When he stopped talking and started kissing, I broke it off and cupped his face. "I don't care if it's a shack in the middle of the stream. I'll love it because it's yours."

His eyes warmed over, and he grinned. "Good. Because it's a part of me, and you're stuck with me now, whether or not you like it."

I rose up on tiptoe and kissed his dimple, just like I'd wanted to do when we first met. Had that really only been days ago? It felt as if he'd been in my life...well, forever. "Even when I leave?"

"Especially then." He hugged me so tight I gasped for breath, and I loved every second of it. "I'll be here. Waiting for you. I'll always be waiting for you."

"And I'll always be yours."

I giggled when he licked my neck, then nibbled on my skin. As long as he was mine and I was his, we could do anything. And I knew, deep down to the bottom of my soul, this would be my happy ending. This is what little girls hoped for, as they grew up watching all those fairy tales. This was real.

And I couldn't be happier.

Epilogue

Mackenzie
Three months later

C tugged my cowboy hat lower, watching the man on the small stage. He was singing in a way that made my whole body tingle and come to life. He had a one-of-a-kind voice, the kind that stayed with you forever and ever and never let you go. It was like an orgasm for your ears. He was that good.

And he was all mine.

Women all over the room watched him, but he didn't even look down at them. His eyes were closed. He sang so clearly. So perfectly. He strummed his guitar, playing the last chords for the song he'd written for me. I made him sing it to me in bed every once in a while. It was too gorgeous *not* to. I'd written lots of songs, but I'd never had one written for me.

He leaned into the mic again.

"You came into my life, never knowing what you'd do.

Not knowing that by the time you were done, I'd feel you through and through.

Love isn't something you can buy or steal.

It's something you have to fight to feel...

And I never have, until you."

He played the last three chords, then stood there, his eyes shut for a minute. I feasted my eyes on him before I crept backward, out the door. That was his last song. It was always his last song. And I had to exit before he saw me. He didn't know I was here, and I wanted to keep it that way. It was a surprise.

He'd been making my life a fairy tale these past few months. Flowers, chocolates, and little gifts came to the campus at least once a week. I'd been sending him stuff, too, and we FaceTimed every night. Spent hours talking about our dreams and hopes. I'd even been flying down to see him almost every weekend, up until finals started. Then life had gotten too hectic, and I'd missed him like crazy.

But that was finally over.

The quarter was over, and well, I still felt the same way I had a few months ago. If anything, I felt even more. As a matter of fact, I was going to tell him I loved him tonight. We hadn't said those three little words yet, but I was fairly certain he felt the same way about me. At least, I hoped so.

"You're here early."

I jumped, pressing a hand to my chest. I turned around, smiling at Austin's little sister, Rachel. She'd been watching him sing, too, apparently. I don't know how I'd missed her. "Yeah. I wanted to surprise him, so I didn't let him know. Why are you at a bar?"

"Austin let me listen from the back room. Don't worry—I had a babysitter watching me the whole time."

I rolled my eyes. "Mrs. Greer?"

Rachel nodded, smiling at me. "I think I'll catch a ride home with her and sleep over at Kaitlyn's tonight. Give you two some freedom to...well, you know."

"You don't have to leave," I protested. "I want to see you, too."

"Aw, I love you, too." Rachel grinned and hugged me. "But I'll see you plenty tomorrow, after you two have some *alone* time." She squeezed my shoulder. "He's been moping around lately, looking all depressed. He needs a night with you where he doesn't have to worry about me."

Oh, crap. That didn't sound good. "Why has he been upset?"

"I think he misses you." Rachel shrugged. "I dunno. I don't speak male."

I laughed. "All right. Movies tomorrow?"

Rachel nodded and pulled out her phone. "Sure. We can see the latest Nicholas Sparks film if you want."

"Sounds good."

We said our goodbyes, hugging, then I walked around the back of the bar. I texted Austin as I walked. *How'd it go?*

Good. Full house again.

I grinned. *Awesome. I can't wait to see you.*

Same here. Only one more week, right?

Right. I'd reached the door where he would be coming out. Luckily, I'd beaten him there, even with me stopping to chat with Rachel. So, I leaned against the wall, lifting a knee and trying to look all casually sexy. Hopefully I pulled it off.

My heart raced when I heard a shuffling sound from behind the steel door. It had been a month since we last saw each other. I'd been wrapped up in finals and studying, and he'd been wrapped up in being a father figure to Rachel. It had been a long freaking month. The back door opened, and he came out, his usual Redskins hat pulled down low on his head.

He had his phone in his hand, and his head was lowered over it. He skipped down the step, whistling between his teeth. It was my song. I smiled. "Hey there, sexy."

He stopped walking, his eyes scanning the alley. "Mac? Is that you?"

"Who else would be calling you sexy?"

He laughed. "I've heard the word used to describe me a few times."

"I'm sure you have. I came down early to surprise you." I pushed off the wall, walking toward him slowly. "I have something I have to tell you. I couldn't wait another second."

"All right." He swallowed hard, tugging his hat lower. He did that when he was nervous. I knew that about him. I also knew he'd been taking night classes at the local college. I was so proud of him for that, and I knew he was, too—even though he kept downplaying it as if it wasn't a big deal. "I've noticed you've been quiet lately. If you changed your mind about coming down here…?"

I faltered. "What makes you think that? Have you changed your mind?"

"What? No." He tugged his hat again, then shoved his hands in his pockets. "I just know it's been a while, and things change. People change. You might have decided you're better off in Chicago, and that's okay. I get it."

"That didn't change." I shook my head. Was this why he'd been reserved lately, like Rachel said? He thought I might have changed my mind about us? Yeah. Not happening. "Only one thing has changed between us."

He nodded. "Okay. What is it?"

"I'm going on tour soon, and it's summer."

"I know." He cocked his head. "You sent me your schedule last week."

"Yeah, but…I'd like you and Rachel to come with me." I took a deep breath and straightened my back. "As a matter of fact, I'd like you to open for me, if you'd be interested in doing so."

He paled, even in the dim lighting of the moon. "That's really nice of you, but I don't—"

"You can totally do this, Austin." I closed the distance between us, resting my hands on his chest. "I know you can. There might be some guilt over what happened when you were in L.A., and you might not want be in the eye of the paparazzi,

139

but that doesn't mean you can't sing. The world deserves to hear you. To know you."

"But—" He broke off and let out a frustrated sound. "I hate this fucking hat," he muttered, taking it off my head and tossing it to the side. "There's that's better. I can actually see you now."

"Fine. Please say yes?"

He covered my hands with his own, looking down at me with those blue eyes that never stopped haunting me, even in my sleep. His dimple was shadowed from the streetlights, and I reached up on tiptoe to kiss it. His eyes fluttered closed, but his grip on me didn't loosen. "Why is it so important to you that I do this? Why do you want me to be heard so badly?"

"Because I know the world will love you." I bit down on my lip, then blurted out, "They'll love you as much as I do. Because I do. I love you, Austin. I love you so much I can't even imagine a life without you in it."

His eyes went wide. "Thank fucking God."

He kissed me, his mouth moving over mine as he hugged me close, seeming like he'd never let go. And I didn't want him to. I never wanted to let him go. My life was so much brighter with him in it. I was different with him. Better.

He said I made him better too. I wasn't sure if that was possible, but it sounded nice. By the time he dragged his mouth away from mine, I had my arms around his neck, urging him closer. I tried to kiss him again, but he shifted just out of reach.

"Wait. It's my turn to talk now. You had yours."

A laugh bubbled out of me. "Hey. Those were my words."

"I know." He nuzzled my neck. "And they worked on me, so they better work on you."

I huffed out a breath and curled my fists into his shirt. "It works."

"Good. Otherwise that would've been really awkward." He kissed the tip of my nose, then sobered up. "You really love me?"

"I really do. I think I have since the first time you kissed me, but it took me this long to be sure. I didn't want to rush into anything, or rush you into anything before you were ready." I trailed a finger over his jawline, smiling at the stubble that scraped my skin. "But for me, it's always been you. Even before I knew you, I was waiting for you."

He groaned and hugged me close, squeezing me until a little squeak escaped. "I love you too. So damn much. It scares the hell outta me, and so do you, quite frankly, but I love you more than I ever thought I could love someone besides Rachel."

I smiled so big that it hurt my face. It was *that* kind of smile. "Thank God." I let out a nervous laugh. "I was scared you weren't there yet."

"Oh, I'm so fucking there that I already have a house built on that road." He laughed, loud and clear, and then spun me in a circle. I clung to him, holding on for dear life. "So you're actually moving down here with me?"

"Hell yeah I am." I removed his hat and tossed it with mine. If he got to take mine off, then I got to do the same to him. I buried my fingers in his soft brown hair, knowing life didn't get any sweeter than this. "I'm all yours, baby."

He nuzzled my neck. "I'll go on tour with you, and I'll sing, too. But only if Rachel is okay with it. I have to talk to her first."

Triumph soared through me, quick and heady. "Touring the country all summer with her favorite singers in the world? Yeah. I'm sure she'll say no."

He laughed. God, I loved his laugh. "Cocky, much?"

"Yep. And you *like* me this way."

He threw his arm over my shoulder, leading us over to where we'd thrown our hats. As we settled them both in place, trying to hide from the world, he grinned down at me. "How about we grab a few drinks before heading home?"

I rested my head on his arm, as best as I could with the big hat on my head. "I like the sound of that. I could go for some Sex on the Beach."

"I can handle that, but we're walking the wrong way." He pointed over his shoulder. "The beach is that way."

I hit his arm, laughing. "You know what I mean."

"I do," he admitted. "But we could always have both versions."

"Last time we did that, the photos were all over the news."

He winced. "Those might have been the first pictures to hit the news, but they're certainly not the last ones."

He was right. Our faces had been plastered all over the news for the past three months. Anytime we went out, the cameras were there waiting for us. Hopefully we managed to get through tonight in privacy. I'd travelled under a false name.

I wrapped my arm around his waist, holding on tight. "Quinn and Cassie forward me all the articles when they see them. I swear to God they have a Google alert on us."

"That's what friends are for," Austin said, grinning.

I laughed. "Yeah, maybe. Either way, at least we're in this together, right?"

"Right." He kissed my temple. "I wouldn't have it any other way, sweetheart."

"Yeah. Me neither."

And then I kissed him.

Want more Sex on the Beach?

BEYOND ME
By Jennifer Probst

CAN FUN IN THE SUN TURN INTO LASTING LOVE?

Spring break in Key West with my besties was supposed to be casual fun. But I never expected to meet *him*. Sex and frolic? Yes! A relationship? No. But his hot blue eyes and confident manner drew me in. And when he let me see the man behind the mask, I fell hard, foolishly believing there could be a future for us. Of course, I never considered our relationship might be based on lies...or that his betrayal could rock my foundation and make me question everything I believed in...

OR WILL A LIFE BUILT ON LIES RUIN EVERYTHING?

The moment I saw her I knew I had to have her. She hooked me with her cool eyes and don't-touch-me attitude. I had it all—money, social status, and looks. I could get any girl I wanted...until her. When my friends challenged me with a bet to get her into bed by the end of the week, I couldn't pass it up. But sex wasn't supposed to turn into love. She wasn't supposed to change me, push me, and make me want more for myself. She wasn't supposed to wreck me in all ways. And now, if I can't turn my lies into truth, I just might lose her forever...

BEFORE YOU
By Jenna Bennett

It's all fun and games

I had a simple plan for spring break.

Sun, sand, and a hot guy. Sex on the beach with no strings attached.

A chance to get rid of this pesky virginity once and for all.

And when I met Tyler McKenna, I thought I had it made.

Until someone gets hurt

But then girls started turning up at Key West landmarks. Girls who looked like me, but with one crucial difference: They'd all been drugged and relieved of their virginity.

The virginity I still have. The virginity Ty refuses to take.

And now I've begun to wonder whether there isn't more to him than meets the eye.

Suddenly, sex on the beach doesn't sound so good anymore...

Other Books by Jen McLaughlin

Out of Line Series

Out of Line
Out of Time
Out of Mind coming 2014

Written as Diane Alberts:

Take a Chance Series

Try Me (Take a Chance #1)
Love Me (Take a Chance #2)
Play Me (Take a Chance #3)
Take Me (Take a Chance #4)

Faking It
Divinely Ruined
On One Condition
Broken
Kiss Me At Midnight

Superstars in Love Series

Captivated by You
One Night

About the Author

Jen McLaughlin is a New York Times, USA Today, and Wall Street Journal bestselling author. She writes steamy new adult books for the young and young at heart. Her first release, Out of Line, came out September 2013. She also writes bestselling contemporary romance under the pen name Diane Alberts. Since receiving her first contract offer under the pen name Diane Alberts, she has yet to stop writing. She is represented by Louise Fury at The Bent Agency.

Though she lives in the mountains, she really wishes she was surrounded by a hot, sunny beach with crystal-clear water. Though she lives in the mountains, she really wishes she was surrounded by a hot, sunny beach with crystal-clear water. She lives in Northeast Pennsylvania with her four kids, a husband, a schnauzer mutt, a cat, and a Senegal parrot. In the rare moments when she's not writing, she can usually be found hunched over one knitting project or another. Her goal is to write so many well-crafted romance books that even a non-romance reader will know her name.

This paperback interior was designed and formatted by

CPSIA information can be obtained
at www.ICGtesting.com
Printed in the USA
FFHW020656300419
52170999-57534FF